The Storyteller's Quilt

Beginnings Are Boundless

SHERRY LYNN CAMPBELL

The Storyteller's Quilt
Beginnings Are Boundless

Copyright © 2025 by Sherry Lynn Campbell

RHG Media Production
21519 Knoll Way,
Castro Valley, CA 94546.

ISBN Paperback: 979-8-9991417-0-5
ISBN Hardcover: 979-8-9991417-1-2

Visit us on line at www.YourPurposeDrivenPractice.com
Published in the United States of America.

What People Are Saying

"Each chapter will awaken something inside you. The stories are real, rich, and full of heart. I was reminded how deeply connection matters, and how much wisdom is available in our everyday lives."
—**Gary L. Fretwell**, Fretwell Solutions

$$\cdot \bullet \bullet \bullet \cdot$$

"True to its title, *The Storyteller's Quilt* is a patchwork of short stories. Each story is a gem in its own right (in one case, literally), and together they form the glittering tapestry."
—**Craig Young**

$$\cdot \bullet \bullet \bullet \cdot$$

"This book immediately captured my attention. The characters are stitched together in a magical way, much like a colorful quilt."
—**Kathleen Frazer**
Jewelry Designer, Quilt Crafter, New Zone Gallery

$$\cdot \bullet \bullet \bullet \cdot$$

"Sherry Campbell has crafted a beautiful novel filled with strong, compelling characters who journey through both familiar and fantastical landscapes."
—**Janet Hall**
Chief Financial Officer, Stanford Alumni Association

· • ● · ·

"*The Storyteller's Quilt* is a winding narrative with lots of twists and turns to keep you captivated."
—**Becky Moller**

· • ● · ·

"*The Storyteller's Quilt* twists and turns, weaving widely varying patches of adventure together in an earnest frame. It's a stitching together that puts love first, despite the complexities of the society."
—**Jay Fry**

A Letter to the Reader

My earliest memories of family and community and of a world bigger than myself centered around storytelling. As an individual, I have always been captivated by the storyteller's voice, the cadence of their words, and so on. Opening a book for me was akin to opening up a door into another world where I could visit whenever I opened that door.

For centuries, people and communities have been coming together to hear a new story, a revised old story or one told exactly the same way throughout the ages, and yet every time one hears it, there is always a surprise—something new to be learned and understood.

I knew from the very first story I ever heard that someday I would be the storyteller. I've lived every day with that as my purpose. My purpose is to share these stories with you. May they enrich your life as they have mine.

From my storyteller's heart to yours.

Enjoy.

Sherry

THIS WORK IS DEDICATED TO:

THE CHILD WHO NEVER CEASES TO SEE WONDER

AND TO

THE WARRIOR WHO BEFRIENDS CHANGE

AND TO

THE MOTHER WHO CARES FOR US BY ALLOWING
US OUR OWN TEMPO

AND TO

THE CRONE WHO TEACHES US WITH PATIENCE,

SO THAT I CAN FIND THE WISDOM IN IT ALL

I THANK YOU

Dedication

Each story included in this book, that Forbes dreams, is a story written as I grew in my own life. Therefore, to me, they are the quilt squares of my life.

Each story has a dedication to the people who have been and are still a part of my life and world as I continue to grow, learn and expand in an eddy of Love.

Beginnings are Boundless is dedicated to my Mother and Father, my first birthday present from God. I love you.

Once Upon a Time is dedicated to my love and husband, Michael. I will always find you. I will always remember your eyes.

The Christmas Wish is dedicated to Marjorie and Bob Variel for the unexpected wonder of love in finding you, my adopted grandparents.

The Easy Way Out is dedicated to anyone who has ever had the courage to change their life for the better of themselves.

The Guardian and the Gate is dedicated to all who have been my mentors.

Opalessence is dedicated to the magic of Love.

Childom is dedicated to my son, Brenden. Thank you for blessing me with your choice and I am forever grateful for your guidance as my navigator.

Table of Contents

"Everything in the Universe has a purpose. Indeed, the invisible intelligence that flows through everything in a purposeful fashion is also flowing through YOU."

—Dr. Wayne W. Dyer

Beginnings Are Boundless

———— ··•·· ————

I n the beginning, there are only beginnings. But everything must have a birth. There is nothing unique about the idea, only the fact that everything starts somewhere. I don't remember my beginning. I only remember being, and along my journey, the realization of who or what I am and can be. From my point of view, I am presently at my beginning, because it is here, at this point in my existence, that I will actually choose to take a form to become something different than what I have been. I can choose anything...for, you see, beginnings are boundless in their possibilities.

I need only look around and explore my own preferences as to what and who I will be henceforth. It is not a choice to make lightly, but rather one made with much consideration. Therefore, I feel my beginning is of significant importance to the whole of existence. It is that thought which moves me to chronicle the choice of my becoming.

Quiet. Can you hear it? The stillness in which the birth of my chosen beginning moment opens...it is at last my moment to become. I pause. From this point on, control over my newly chosen existence will be fleeting at best. Deep breath. Calmness. I will trust my judgment and, with confidence, I make my choice.

—A Being

Part I

A lone cart rumbles down a lonely road. It is near dusk. The driver of the cart sighs. The tired beast pulling the cart sighs. The driver knows he can go no farther in the coming darkness, and that his beast needs rest and food. He looks from side to side of the road. No place on either side seemed to offer any sense of hospitality or shelter from the roadside. He cast his gaze ahead, up the road, and saw nothing more promising looking up there. Sighing, he clicks his tongue and pulls the reins towards the right, steering the beast and his cart off the lonely road to an even more lonely campsite.

He sighs deeply as he sits in his now motionless cart. He is very tired. The loud grumblings of his beast stir him from his momentary daze. "Yes, yes," he mutters to the animal. After lowering himself off the cart, he stretches a long stretch, trying to get the blood moving once more through his body. He stiffly walks around to the back of the cart and proceeds to set about making camp. He sees to the needs of his laboring beast first, food and water. He chuckles at the appreciation and gratitude he imagines seeing in the animal's eyes. When one has no human company, one can easily turn to an animal for companionship.

"Humph. Not much wood around, even for kindling," he mutters to himself. Another sigh. He goes back into the cart's wagon and pulls forth a heavy burlap-wrapped parcel. He pinches up his nose as he unwraps the contents. Dung. He swallows hard. Oh well, it burns hot and long. It's better than a cold night with no fire. Besides, he knows he'll get used to the smell after a few minutes. It is the sorting through the not-so-dry pieces to find the hard, dry ones that is so distasteful. There isn't even a stream nearby to wash. Water is a resource not to be wasted needlessly. He shrugs. Guess good 'ole dirt will have to do the trick tonight. He wants to find some sort of makeshift utensil to eat with though, instead of relying on his hands.

All in all, he felt pretty content that he makes do with his lot in life. He has a lot more than other people. He has clothing, food, water, a beast and a cart. But what he is most proud of is his ingenuity. He'd discovered long ago that everything has a purpose. A use. One might have to look very closely to find that use, but it is always there. And he always found it.

The dreary sky is now completely dark. His stomach is full and his body recovering from the strain of a day of travel over an uneven road on an unforgiving wooden bench. His small, but warm, dung fire is glowing cheerfully in the surrounding gloom. By using his cart as a makeshift shelter, he and his beast feel relatively safe. As safe as anyone could feel, knowing any passerby could easily see their camp. He grimaces and scratches his face. Funny that he'd not seen more travelers on this road. He scratches his face again, realizing that the next stream he finds meant a bath and a shave. He leans back into his makeshift pillow, a blanket stuffed with clothes, propped up against the cartwheel for support and stretches out his legs beside the small fire. Where is he traveling to? When he started out a week or so ago from his last stopover, he had known. It had been very clear. But now, as he tries to relax after a day of travel and plan for tomorrow, he realizes he has no inkling of where he is headed or why. He moves restlessly against his pillow, trying to find a truly comfortable position. Giving up, he pulls his legs in to sit cross-legged. He leans forward, elbows on knees and stares into the dung flames. "Where am I going?" he asks himself.

This is a terribly perplexing question for him. He knows that everything and every action has a purpose, a use. And the longer he sits in front of this small dung fire, the more any purpose or use for this trip escapes him. The very thought shakes him to his soul. He has for so long based his entire existence on this belief and now.... Now, he feels very small, very alone, very insignificant, and for the very first time, unsure. He is, in truth, scared.

He makes a face and spits into the fire. How could he sleep now? He is truly exhausted. He looks over at his beast. His beast seems peaceful and relaxed enough. He sighs a frustrated sigh. "I think too much," he says to the beast. The beast slightly turns its head towards him and opens its eyes to look at him, momentarily. Then, because the man speaks no more, turns away and continues to chew, and chew, and chew its hay. In an expression of defeat, he leans back into his makeshift pillow, pulls his blanket over himself, closes his eyes, forbidding his mind to think any more on the subject, and he wills himself to sleep.

I am aware. Therefore, I am alive. Okay, now what? I have a body. I can sense that but it doesn't seem to answer my will. I try to see through my eyes but my vision is impaired. I am flawed? Why can't I move? I know that I am cold. I will speak so someone will attend to me. I concentrate and instruct my voice to cry out for assistance but, that sound?? The sound I hear with my own ears is not a voice, but rather a wail! I have no voice?? Something must have gone terribly wrong. Try to stay calm. Think. THINK!

I made a choice to put my existence into form. I studied many different forms before I chose the one I felt most compatible with my ambitions. But, I do not think this is right! I chose human. THIS does not feel human!

··●··

The Carter is awakened by the most dreadful wail he's ever heard. He opens his eyes, but doesn't move. He is disoriented. Where is he? Oh yea, on a lonely road going somewhere he is unclear of at the moment. There it is again! That sound! Is it a local haunt looking for a soul to torment? He shudders under his dew-damp blanket. He looks over at his beast, "What do you see?" he whispers. The beast brays loudly. The man takes that response as "Nothing." Wonderful, he thinks to himself. What a way to start a sure-to-be-absolutely-dreadful day. Summoning the courage he doesn't directly feel, he slowly gets up, wrapping his blanket around him for warmth. There is no sun yet, only a thick gray-lighted fog indicating it's dawn. The sound rings out again. He turns sharply to his right. It's coming from that direction. He can feel his heart pounding, and sense his breath quickening. Quickly, he throws off his blanket and moves to the back of his cart. He looks around in the wagon for anything that would suffice as a weapon. He finds an extra brake handle he had made from a branch found on the road. With the handle firmly grasped in one hand, he hits it against his other hand, testing both his grip and the strength of the wood. Good enough. He looks up from the wagon, listening for the sound.

The noise has a wavering pattern to it: one minute the wailing is earth-shattering loud, then it tapers off into a kind of gurgling. It maintains a stable position, not seeming to move closer or further away. The sound didn't seem to come from any other direction. Perhaps it is a wounded animal? If so, he'd have fresh meat and a hide to sell. With hopes of finding something useful and potentially profitable, he sets off, feeling sure to find a prize.

He follows the sound. He really couldn't apply a great deal of stealth to the affair, since there are no trees or shelter of any kind anywhere to disguise his approach. With every step, the sound becomes increasingly louder. He moves into what he thinks is his battle-stance crouch. He narrows his eyes and hones his senses to any and all sounds around him. He tightens his grip on the stick, which is slipping a little due to the extra supply of perspiration he is producing in his palms. Using his tongue, he wets his lips. He tries to walk very quietly. The fog is hampering his long-range vision, but he knows he is close. The sound is so loud. He slowly raises the stick up above his head, ready to strike if needed. And then, all of a sudden, he comes upon the wailing creature! A baby?

He looks down in total disbelief at this screaming and flailing infant. He relaxes his arm and lowers the stick. He stands up out of his crouch. He blinks. Then he looks down once more at the wailing baby. "What on earth are you doing out here, naked no less, in the middle of nowhere?" he asks aloud, not expecting any answer of course. He is, nonetheless, quite shocked to find the baby's wailings and flailing grow more intense at the voicing of his question. He drops his stick. Oh my god! A baby! Instinct takes over. Instinct to save a life, to protect the helpless and to give meaning to being. He picks up the child. UGGH! It is filthy. But that wasn't really the child's fault. So, he thinks, if I can dig through dung for a fire, I can handle this. A feeling of great importance surges through him. This is a profound moment in his life. For the very first time in his life, that he can remember, someone needs him, really needs him. With a smile, he purposefully walks back to his beast and cart, taking great care in holding the fragile, precious baby. His baby.

I am exhausted from this whole experience. I could have just stayed as I was, even though it was a really poor excuse for existence, but at least I had some shred of dignity. And some control! Here, and now, I am helpless. And in further examination of my choice processes, I realize I had only studied adult forms—not forms from their beginnings. What a flawed plan! And now, now I am stuck. I don't know what is more infuriating: being trapped, or not being able to rant around and complain about my present situation.

At last! Some assistance! Well??? I can tell you are there. I can't see you clearly, but I can hear you. Are you just planning on hovering there or are you going to do something to help me? Sigh. He seems so unsure. How difficult can it be? Pick me up and clean me off and make me warm! And I'm hungry, so please feed me. Of course, my thoughts are only translating into louder and more frantic wailing noises rather than concise language. I do have to admit that my limbs do seem to be moving quite vigorously in tune with my wailing.

OOOH! The sense of being picked up is nauseating. He holds me out and away from his body and the sense of suspension in mid-air is terrifying. The man seems somewhat intelligent though. He heard my sounds and found me. He seems to know I want to be cared for, and now he is holding me closer to his body. AAAH! The warmth of his body as he cradles me close is a very welcome sensation. I have never experienced touch before. Touch is nice. A happy sigh. Maybe my experience wouldn't be all so bad. A strange feeling is permeating throughout my body. It's contentment. Instinct takes over, instinct to trust to be loved and to love in return, to live. I smile inside my new form. I have never had anyone to care for or anyone to care for me. I have never needed anyone. I need this man. I only hope that he needs me too. For the moment, I feel safe.

He approaches his little camp quickly. The beast is watching him. "A baby," he says to the animal as he walks past it to kneel beside a barely smoldering fire. He grabs his hastily discarded blanket, bunches it up a little for cushioning, then places the baby atop it. He grabs some stuffing out of his makeshift pillow, a shirt, and covers the baby. He gets up and goes to the dung bag. He needs to remake his fire. He needs to heat water. His precious water. But the baby needs to be cleaned. And fed! "What do you feed a baby?" he asks absently. He looks over at his beast. He imagines he sees the animal's questioning eyes ask, "What are you looking at me for?" So, of course he responds to both himself and to the beast with, "Do you think you can produce any milk today?" The beast brays in protest.

He walks over to face his cow. "Okay, so I know it's been a long time since you produced milk, but you were a cow first before you pulled carts," he explains to the animal in hopes of convincing her to help him. He is not accustomed to going against the will of others, man or beast. The animal shifts her body weight, which he interprets as affirmation of his requests. "Thank you," he says to his animal. And in an uncharacteristic display of affection to his trusted companion, he leans forward, throwing his arms around her neck, then kisses her between her eyes. As he stands up, the animal lowers her head and leans gently into the man. "I know," he says, patting her brow, as tears fill his eyes and a thickness forms in his throat. He takes a deep breath, pulls his shoulders back and then gets busy.

To his own surprise, he is doing great. A happy little dung fire is going, the water is near boiling. He has coaxed enough milk from his dear, dear cow for the baby's meal, and the baby is no longer crying. After the water boils, he lets it cool, while making preparations to bath the infant. It is covered and caked in dirt as well as with its own waste. Happily, he washes the dirty little face. It is a good little face...almost too beautiful for a boy. That stray thought stops him. The sex. Actually, he hadn't even noticed the sex of the child. What if it wasn't a boy? Oh, god. He looks at the child, who is looking up at him, and panic hits. How would he handle a girl? He takes a deep breath. He dunks the washing rag into the hot water. He squeezes out the excess water from the washing rag. Heavy sigh. He goes to work bathing the baby's genital area. His fear flares before him, bright as a shooting star. The baby is a girl. His heart sinks. Tears flow down his face. He continues his washing. He continues to cry. He doesn't know anything about girls. He would have nothing to offer this girl. His newly found usefulness is fading away, even as the last wisps of the morning fog are burning off. The first town or community he showed up in would take her away. A man can't raise a girl-child. It just wasn't done, even when the paternal father is involved. If the mother dies, the girl-child is taken away to a female relative or a foster mother.

He was bathing her, both with water and with his tears. He looks down at this small, helpless girl-baby. Her eyes are open and watching him. He wonders how much babies can understand. He thinks he sees a lot more intelligence in those eyes than should be there, but he reminds himself that he has an active imagination. "They won't let me keep you," he says to her. And as he covers her up with his old shirt, taking care to wrap her snugly for warmth, he cries at the loss he feels and for the lost chance to be needed.

Warmth. Soft. Whatever he put me on is a lot nicer than whatever I was lying on before. My eyes seem to be responding better to my demands for sight. My body's inability to have a wide range of motion also inhibits my range of vision. I can see the man moving with great purpose about his little camp. Does he live here? How dreadful his station in this life must be. Hmmm. Why does he talk to his cow? Does he think the cow will answer him? I chose to become man because of his ability to communicate intelligently with other men. Was I misled in my judgment of other species? The cow didn't seem to respond verbally to the man, but the cow did seem to understand and answer his queries. Curious.

Absently, I realize I have stopped making that dreadful wailing noise. Thank goodness. I thought I might go mad listening to myself.

I try to follow the man's movements around the camp. He's moving too fast for this immature body to keep up with. Heavy sigh. At least I'm comfortable. Ugh! What is that awful smell?? He's kneeling over something. He's making fog? No. I can feel the heat now. He must be making a fire, but what on earth is he burning that would smell so dreadful? Don't think about it, just enjoy the warmth.

He looks like he's preparing to cook a meal. I am so hungry. Almost as if he can hear my thoughts, he turns to me. He gently lifts my head and spoons water into my mouth. Oh, yes! That's nice. Very good. He puts my head back down. I hope that's not all I'm getting; water will only quench my thirst, not my hunger. On cue, he turns his attention back to me. He once again lifts my head, and this time spoons a kind of warm mush into my mouth. I want to protest at his choice of cuisine, but my little body needs nourishment in order to flourish. I accept his food offerings as graciously as possible. He is tender in his attentions to me. I am thankful for his company.

He lays my head back down and moves away from me. He returns presently with intentions other than feeding. At last, bath time. He lifts off the material covering me. Burr. It's cold. But I'm not going to complain. He probably hates the sound of my wailing as well.

Oh! What a wonderful feeling to be clean. Warm water on my face is wonderful, and that rubbing thing that gets the dirt off feels great. Oh, the man is very kind. When I can teach this body to speak, I will be sure to thank him for all his kindness. My eyes are watching him. He seems very happy. What...? What's wrong? His face has changed. He's stopped cleaning. He's contemplating something, something serious by the look on his face. He gets the cleaning cloth wet again, and with a very different expression, he starts at his task again. He is cleaning the more personal areas of the human body now. Maybe I'm missing something? With all the other things that have seemed to go wrong with this beginning of mine, why shouldn't there be more flaws?

He's crying now. He is still washing me, but with distraction rather than tender attention. Oh, what is wrong you silly man?? Won't you speak to me? And then I hear him say, "They won't let me keep you."

With that statement, I know my flaw. Yep, when I make a miscalculation, I do it with greatness. What a dreadful day.

I had chosen to become man. I fully expected to become an adult male. My initial expectation of having "fleeting control at best" has been realized to the utmost. Beginnings are indeed boundless in their possibilities. I have begun my beginning as an infant female in a world where females are kept separated from society, reserved for very specific tasks, and considered less valuable than this man's cow.

And yet, this man cries for me. I cannot even cry for myself. How long do humans live? Maybe I'll die soon and I can try this over and get it right? No, that's beyond my available options at the moment. It'd be at least three or four years before I would have the coordination to kill myself. But I know, even if I had the ability this moment, I wouldn't go through with it. I am no quitter. Obviously, I'm a rotten planner though. Sigh.

I look up at this man, I try to put all the tenderness and understanding I can into my eyes to let him know, "We'll get through this if we help each other." He continues to cry, but I think I see understanding glimmer in his eyes.

Everything has a purpose, a reason. He is more sure of that than ever. He couldn't get over the look in the eyes of this little baby girl. He knows she knows what is going on here. He wipes his tears on the back of his hand. His doubts from the previous night are all gone. He might not have known where he was going to, but he knows why he had come here—to find this baby, to become her protector and for him to have a purpose in a world that did not realize he existed. He would not let this opportunity be taken from him. He would raise her as he would raise a son. He would teach her how to be masculine and hide her true sex. He would give her a male name. A name. "A name?" he says aloud to himself. Hmmm. What would he name her?

A name like everything else should have a purpose, a meaning. Obviously her name couldn't be a feminine one. He needs a strong name for her. A name that would, by its very nature, protect her. He turns and looks away into the distance at nothing, absently scratching his upper lip. He sighs.

He is still sitting beside the cozy little fire. The day is progressing along, most of the morning gloom gone. The now clean baby has snuggled deep into the makeshift cradle beside him. He looks down at her. He finds it strange that her eyes never seem to leave him.

Well, he's got potential! If there is anyone who will help me, it's this old man. He seems to be struggling with his own thoughts though. I wish he'd continue to talk to me. I can't read his thoughts! Calm down. If I stare at him long enough, he'll get the picture that there's something more profound going on here than meets the eye, the ordinary eye. "A name." He said 'a name.' Sigh! I can relax now. He'd not be worrying about a name if he wasn't going to help me. He is obviously as aware as I regarding the status of females in this society and by his actions, he seems not to be in agreement with all of his societal obligations and regulations. Well, at least if I am going to make a mistake, I am provided a protector until a solution provides itself. And, now that I think of it, what is this man doing way out here? There's obviously nothing worth traveling out here for, unless...

A shiver runs through me. There's something else at work here besides me! But, what? Or whom?

Oh! He's finally looking at me again! I guess my staring is good for something.

"You know what's going on here, don't you?" he asks the baby. He must be crazy talking to a baby and thinking that the baby could understand, but he knows she does. So he continues on with his discussion, one-sided as it is, "Well, here's the situation little one. We have a problem. I'm a man and you're a female. Here and now, men cannot raise girl-children. Females are kept separate from our main society. The reasons are so old that I cannot even remember them completely, but not remembering the original reason doesn't change the Law. There are rebels in the land who do not agree with the Law and are trying to force changes. These rebels believe male and female should live together in 'family units.' Well, that's the term they use anyway. I don't care much one way or another for the confines of politics, policies and cities, which is why I travel around on this cart. I try to make my own life my own. There are reasons for the existence of everything. I mostly find things, figure out how they are useful and then utilize them. So, it makes perfect sense to me that I found you. Of course, figuring out what you're good for may take some time. But I know beyond any doubt that there was, is, a reason that I found you. And the feelings you've stirred in me are new. I want to explore them and make them useful. I want to have a purpose, a use. Presently, that use is to care for you, to protect you."

He pauses, wondering how to go on. He looks down into the girl's face. The baby is very still and focuses on him. Her eyes follow his words and his facial expressions. However impossible it seems, she is intently listening to him and understanding what he says. He sighs again. What an odd trip this has turned out to be.

"So here's what I think," he begins again, "I have to disguise you so that you will appear male. I have to discover a name for you that is masculine but does not hide your soul. A name that will give you power in this world and misdirect those who would not allow you to live free. And you have to understand that I do not value you less because of your gender. And," he pauses here for a moment, then continues, "you also have to understand that if we are discovered, we will both be killed. No exceptions." He pauses again, looks straight into her eyes, and continues. "I could kill you now, and you'd never have to worry about the risks. I could turn you over to the Law, and you could live within their walls. But I'd rather have some company in my life other than my beast. I'd like to have someone to whom I could teach all the things I know. I'd like to know that somehow I made this world a better place by existing. I'd like to know that when I die, I haven't died in truth because someone here loves me and remembers." He is crying now, but he keeps talking and the baby keeps listening. "I want to know if you're willing to take the risk of giving both our lives a meaning, a purpose?"

And, for him, what happens next will always be the most extraordinary thing he has ever experienced; the baby's hand reaches out towards his. He catches his breath, half expecting that it was a baby reflex, but her outstretched hand stays there. Now it's his turn; he reaches his own hand towards hers. Realizing his hand is so much larger than hers, he extends his index finger to her outstretched hand. His finger lightly touches her hand whereupon she reaches a little farther and firmly grasps his finger. The grip is very tight. He looks again into her eyes. He knows she has made her choice. Her choice is to live as a freeman and by his conditions. In that instance, he knows her name as if it had been shouted into his mind.

Her name is Greer.

Part II

The early seasons had been hard on the man. He wasn't as young as he used to be, and raising a baby, turned very active child, took a lot more out of him than he would have expected or liked to admit. But he relished every moment with Greer. It was quite obvious from early on that she was going to be a striking beauty. Though he believed in cleanliness, he tried his best to keep her as dirty as possible, and dressed in clothing at least one size too large. They stayed out of the towns and villages as much as possible. He was a master at living off the land. Well, he always considered it living with the land. Teamwork, he insisted, was the root of success, even if the other team member was seemingly inanimate.

While Greer was growing, he tried to school her in writing, reading, monetary issues, haggling, fighting, the world of politics (at least as much as he understood them), and most importantly how to be a man's man.

At first it was frightfully embarrassing teaching her how to urinate like a man, but with a little help from a carved-out stick, they were able to create a facsimile of the sound and trajectory of a man's urine stream. They simply attached the stick to a leather belt that she wore under her pants. It was painfully uncomfortable for her at first, but with time she learned how to adapt. Like so many other adaptations she had made to create her male illusion, she had had to learn that her life and his now depended on it. He knew that the Law would have forgiven him for a momentary lapse of good judgement in thinking he could raise a girl-child, but after so many seasons they had blatantly and defiantly disobeyed the Law and the social conditions which held his world in order.

The older she got, the more he concentrated on her fighting skills, for he was getting older too. Some nights after their evening meal, he'd sit back against whatever he was using that night for a chair, and simply watch her. Tonight was one of those nights. She was so strong and beautiful. She took his breath away. And, this made him more afraid than anything else in the world. She was approaching her eighteenth season. She'd already passed through her initiation into womanhood. She was nearly as tall as him. She could flatten a grown man with a punch. She was a skilled bowman and swordsman, and more than adequate with a quarter staff. It was only a matter of time before she felt the irresistible urge to find a mate. And, if a man found the truth of her, he'd be helpless but to fall in love with her, and then she'd be caged after all. Even with their carefully laid scheme, he would not be around forever to protect her. His greatest fear was that in the end, she'd be some man's property. He sighed a heavy sigh and looked away from her.

He was only one man, he could not change the world.

And, then a stray thought, like a voice in his mind, said, "*Oh, but you have already.*"

Distracted by the voice in his head, he was surprised when he looked up to see Greer watching him. She had paused in her task of restringing her bow. She simply asked, "Father?"

He looked over at her and smiled a tired smile. "It's nothing Greer," he lied. "I'm simply tired after our match today. You've already surpassed me in strength." He chuckled then, remembering how he almost won their sparring match with that final quarter staff swing, but she countered with a surprise and neatly knocked him off his feet. She moved closer to where he was sitting and joined him on their dirt floor. The fire was very low, but very warm. It had taken years for her to get used to that awful dung smoke, but now that smell meant home. It meant him.

"Yes, well, you better not underestimate me again!" She laughed lightly and gently slapped his knee.

"Where did you come up with that tactic?" he asked. His mood lifting with their conversation.

"I saw it used once and thought it looked handy, so I've been practicing it alone in order to see if it would work. And it did!" Greer said as lightly as she could, knowing the implications of her confession would not go unnoticed.

"Where did you see it used, Greer?" The man who was her father asked as unemotionally as possible. He was struggling to keep his fear and anger at her risk under firm control.

"Well," she paused, "Last turn of the moon or so. I went for a walk one day when you were busy with other tasks." She squirmed in her seated position. Then, obviously agitated, she blurted out, "I was bored Father! I can't remember exactly why I was born, or why I am here, but I know it wasn't to spend this existence in hiding, afraid of all strangers." She stood up and began pacing around their little fire, as if the physical motion of moving helped her get out the emotions she was struggling to express.

He let her speak. He knew it was time. In all their eighteen seasons together, they had never talked about their beginning or their agreement. And slowly as she grew, that knowing, understanding look in her eyes faded and she learned eagerly what he taught her to survive. She always seemed to be fighting against something inside of herself though, a thing she could not touch but knew was there. It was a source of frustration for her. And now, she had to voice it.

"Father, who am I?" There it was. The question he hoped would never come. He waited for the next one, which must follow. "Father, who are you?" He closed his eyes for a moment, then opened them to look across the fire at his beautiful, fully grown girl-child Greer. She met his gaze with the determination of an eager pupil.

"It's such an incredible story, Greer, that you'll think I'm just a silly old man, but you must believe what I tell you is the truth as I know it." Greer relaxed and moved once more closer to the man she loved as her father and sat eagerly beside him to hear the truth.

"It was during the winter season," he began. "I was traveling with my cart and with my beast. I wasn't really heading any one place with more purpose than another. And then, somehow I realized I needed to go somewhere specific. It was a gentle need. So with a destination in mind I headed off to see what I could find. Only, after I got so far along, I lost my purpose. I was frightened. All actions, all things have a purpose. I was the master of discovering those purposes. It was my life's work.

"Anyway, the next morning, I awoke to the most terrible shrieking-wailing noise I have ever heard. I thought it must be an evil spirit sent to carry me away." He paused, taking a sip from his cup, then began again, "But I hoped it was a dying animal I could use for supplies. What I found was you. A baby, laying naked and filthy in the middle of a barren landscape. I had no idea how you'd gotten there, I only knew you needed help. My help. And that finally, after all the searching I had done for the finding of purposes for things, I had finally found a reason, and purpose, for myself.

"So I took you back to my camp. I began to care for your immediate needs. I cleaned you and discovered you were female. I felt my newly found reason to be crash down around me. They would take you away from me. I didn't want them to take you away from me. I wanted to give you everything I knew. I wanted to let you find your true potential. You wouldn't be able to do that if they locked you up in a breeding workhouse. There you are less valuable than my cow!

"But there was something more," he paused, trying to choose his words carefully, "You knew what was going on. You were not just a helpless baby. You were 'YOU' already. Somehow, you understood the peril you were in, and we made an agreement. You chose to live, with me, by my rules, so you could be free. And so our lives began that day as one.

"But the older you grew, when you reached the ages where you could actually vocalize your thoughts, the more that uncanny light of consciousness left your eyes. You became only my beloved Greer. Who you were when you were born disappeared." He stopped and took a slow, shaky breath. There was still one question he had not answered.

"My name is so long forgotten to the world. I have been called the 'Carter' for so many seasons that I no longer know my true name. I was a man with no home, no family, no destination, no true and meaningful purpose until I found you. He looked at her now. He hoped he had given her the information to discover who she was, and where she came from even though he knew the end-purpose of this discovery would be her leaving him.

Greer sat very quietly for a while and stared into the dung fire. She did not know what to say. She only knew that she wanted to remember why she was here.

After what seemed like forever, a silence taut with emotion and questions and fear, Greer finally turned towards the man she called father. "Father, I love you. I think I have always meant to tell you that, as well as to thank you for the care you have given to me. And, not just the care," she paused, "...but the tenderness, and the patience and your unconditional devotion to my well-being." She stopped.

He watched her. He could hear the emotion in her voice and see it in her face and eyes as she looked at him. Then quite extraordinarily, she leaned over and embraced him. In all their seasons together, expressing their emotions through physical contact had been kept to bare necessity. It was his way of maintaining her illusion of masculinity. It was a fierce embrace that said more than any words ever could. And in that moment, he knew that his life's purpose had been fulfilled. He would never truly perish or have lived unnoticed. He had made a choice that had made a difference in the chain of existence. The embrace may have truly only lasted a moment, but for him, it contained a lifetime.

That night, they went to sleep like any other night. In that night, the Carter found his final destination. It was like being nowhere, and yet everywhere at the same time. There was a voice and it said, *"Welcome Home."*

Part III

When Greer awoke the next morning, she knew she was alone. She didn't quite know how she knew, but she knew that the man she had only known as "Father" was dead. She lay under her blankets very still. *I don't want to move. Maybe if I don't move, I will fall back asleep and I'll awake to a different day where Father is still alive. I know it's stupid though. When you die, you die.* Greer took a deep breath, closed her eyes tight, then reopened them to face the gloom of this day.

She wasn't going to charge to meet it though. She sat up, and now remained seated with her blanket wrapped around her, feet drawn up close to her body in order to fit beneath the blanket. She looked past the now heatless dung fire over to the motionless body of her father, still lying beneath his own blanket. She didn't cry. She found that strange that she didn't even want to cry. She just calmly sat and looked at him. The cow mooed and brought her out of her inactivity. She looked over at the beast, "I bet you're hungry, aren't you?" she asked. And with that question, she started her day.

She set about tending to the animal's needs. After that, she moved to restart the dung fire and prepare the morning meal. The season was once again winter, so she had to use what supplies she had sparingly. She moved around the camp as if it were any other morning, carefully stepping over the motionless body under the blanket, but otherwise seemingly not noticing it.

The fire was glowing nice and warm, the smoke filled the air with the sharp, pungent smell she associated with home, and the cow was happily chewing and chewing and chewing. She boiled her morning ration of water and mixed some of the cow's oats into her own bowl for her meal. She ate her breakfast in the silence of the morning fog, which she thought lingered longer than usual.

With breakfast out of the way, she set about breaking camp. It was time for her to move on. She had everything packed neatly in the cart, the way the man had taught her, everything except that one extra precious blanket. She stood and looked at the blanket which lay covering the only person she had ever known but herself. She tilted her head to one side and her eyes got blurry, and an enormous lump swelled in her throat. Her legs buckled beneath her and she found herself sobbing uncontrollably in the dirt. She managed to crawl over to his body and reached out her hand to touch his feet. "Nooooo," she silently mouthed, for no words could get through her swollen, sobbing throat. She laid there, grabbing at his feet until the sun finally burned through the morning gloom.

Part IV

It was a voice in her head that finally pulled her from her despair, *"Get up! Get up! You can't lay here forever! You can't let someone find you like this! Be a man! Get up and bury the body and move on! Live. Live!... and be free..."*

But it wasn't her voice, the one she heard everyday, but a different voice. How can that be? But she didn't have time to ponder all the possibilities, or even impossibilities, the voice was right. She needed to move on. She needed to not be found sobbing like she envisioned a woman might do over a dead man. But she would not be untrue to her love for this man. She would give him a proper burial. A burial like the ones her father had told her of in the stories he had shared with her.

She looked around her. There weren't very many inviting spots to be laid to rest. There weren't even very many trees, so building pyre would be difficult. She chewed on the inside of her lower lip as she wiped away the remaining tears from her face. Then, almost unconsciously she picked up some of the wet dirt she had cried upon and rubbed it onto her face, making her appearance dreadful. She looked over at the cow, who was all strapped up with the cart and ready to move along. She stood up, hands on her hips, and addressed the cow, "What do you think? Do you think dung would work?" The cow brayed and stretched her neck against her harness, then shook to move the harness into a more comfortable position. But after spending so many years with the man, Greer had picked up his habit of reading the animal's behavior as communication of a sort. Greer gently slapped the side of the cow, "Good, we are in agreement. A dung pyre it will be."

Greer spread the remnants of the morning fire out as far as she could, then she pulled the burlap wrapped dung supplies out of her neatly packed cart. She laid out the largest and driest pieces she could find. After replacing the burlap sack, she moved to the next phase. She stood above the body and took a deep breath. Then she bent over and easily picked up the dead man's body, keeping his blanket over him. She laid the body gently upon the bed of dung and rearranged the blanket to cover him. Next, she moved the cow and cart a safe distance away and returned to the site.

She stood beside her pyre, flint stones in hand. She wasn't sure what was supposed to happen next, so she improvised. She raised her arms, hands outstretched above her body and said, "I release this man, Carter, from this life into the great beyond. He is a man whose life will live forever within my life and within the lives of those that shall follow mine. From now and forward, I shall be known to this world, and they shall call me Greer, The Carter."

She bent down and using her flint sparked a flame to engulf her hero's body. What happened next, she would never quite know if it was her grief's vision or reality. The flame quickly engulfed the entire body, and amongst the too large flames, a figure stood and smiled at her. It was her Father. Then as fast as she saw the image, it was gone and the dung smoke filled with the dreadful smell of burning flesh took her choking and coughing away from the pyre.

She sat upon the cart and waited for the flames and smoke to clear away. She jumped off the cart seat and went over the remains of the pyre, but there was nothing left. No ash. No burnt dirt. No nothing. He was gone. With a pensive attitude she returned to the cart, easily swinging herself up into the seat and headed the cow and cart towards the nearest village.

There was so much out there to see and learn. Carter had taught her well. She would heed his teachings. Now was the time to find her purpose. And a voice in her head echoed gently, *"Beginnings are boundless...."*

··●··

CHAPTER 1

Unexpected Visitor

The storyteller's voice trailed off, and after a momentary pause, a loud roar of cheering and hand clapping erupted. The storyteller's eyes were damp as he rose to accept the crowd's approval and appreciation of his story. The emotions of his characters in his stories never failed to be felt by him in the telling.

And as was usual, after a telling, he was exhausted. He graciously made his way out of the gathering hall into the cool and crisp night air. Sleep first then food. He paused, looked up to the stars, putting his hands upon his heart and said "Thank You" out loud. Then he gave a meaningful bow of gratitude. Upon straightening back up into a standing pose, he sighed. As a smile crossed his face, he made his way to his sleeping hut. Again, feeling very grateful for the sleep he knew was coming.

He awoke the next morning to find a serving boy waiting for him. The boy directed him to the relieving station, then bathing, then food. The youth took his job assignment very seriously, and the storyteller had to smile to himself, realizing that he had achieved somewhat of a celebrity status.

In every village or community gathering he attended and shared his stories, he, himself, was always surprised by the enthusiasm that greeted him. He was also continuously surprised by the stories he told. He was never quite sure where they came from. All he knew was that they felt like they were alive in his mind, and each story came out when that story was needed.

Sometimes a story he had previously shared would be requested by someone who had heard him speak at a previous gathering time, but he would always decline. He could not recreate a story. He did not know why. He only knew the story as it unfolded in his mind. He remembered the stories, the characters and the overall theme, but not the specifics. And storytelling needed details.

He was chewing on his bread and cheese breakfast, lost in his own thoughts, when he had the uncomfortable feeling of being watched. He focused his eyes back on his immediate surroundings only to realize that while he had been lost in these thoughts, someone had sat down across from him. A smelly someone, who was staring most directly at him.

He had grown accustomed to people keeping their distance from him, because as much as people enjoyed hearing his stories, no one wanted to be a character in them. And even though he was a young man, the solitary life of a storyteller had suited him. So he was quite surprised indeed by the actions of this young man. He finished chewing, swallowed, took a breath, which he regretted, then as politely as possible asked, "Yes?"

The young man sitting across from him didn't say anything immediately but kept his gaze direct. After a bit of time staring at each other, the young man broke his gaze to look around them to make sure they had relative privacy. The youth assigned to aid the storyteller had been called away for breakfast and kitchen chores. The young man satisfied that they could talk safely, returned his gaze to the storyteller, and in a very measured tone said, "My name is Greer Carter."

The storyteller couldn't breathe, and this time it had nothing to do with the smell of the person sitting across from him. He blinked.

"Did you hear me?" asked Greer.

The storyteller shook his head in an affirmative response. Then managed a question of his own, "Are you 'the' Greer?"

Greer looked at the storyteller and with raised eyebrows said calmly, "Yes."

The storyteller looked around them nervously, understanding the peril of this conversation, then in sort of a conspiratorial pose leaned a bit forward and with a hushed voice asked, "Does anybody know your name?"

"Not here they don't. I don't share my name unless I need to," Greer answered, also using hushed tones.

The storyteller sort of sat back a bit and shook his head, "I don't understand." The storyteller felt like his head was swimming without his body. He felt dizzy. He was out of breath, and it was hard to breathe in. "I don't feel well..." was all he got out before he fell face first into what was left of his breakfast on the table.

Greer moved around the table quickly to pick the man up and get him back to his sleeping hut before the youth returned from his morning chores. Not wanting to make any scene that didn't appear normal, Greer threw one of the storyteller's arms around her shoulder and grabbed him around the waist, gripping his belt to keep him hoisted up against her so that they appeared as two fellows walking together. They got to the hut before the youth could see that two had gone in. And when the youth reappeared, he figured the storyteller had finished breakfast and then returned to his hut for more rest. The youth had fulfilled his morning guest duties, so it was back to the kitchen for him till nightfall.

The storyteller had fallen into a dream. In his dream, a new story unfolds.

··◆··

Once Upon a Time...

Two-fifty p.m. Almost three o'clock. Well, these are the last ten minutes of class for me at the university campus. In one week's time, I will be on my way to Oxford, England and Oxford University for my senior semester abroad. What a dream come true for a language-literature major! I have to be honest with myself though, it is an escape. This last semester couldn't have been worse. I had been the only girl in my circle of friends not to be chosen for a sorority. And then, it was as if my social life, as I had known it, had stopped in its tracks.

That sounds like such a petty matter, but the mere fact of my current situation has crushed my confidence. This coming year would have been my last here anyway, so spending it in a new setting will be refreshing. I believe no one will miss me, not really anyway. This school and campus have become dreadfully small, and I don't fit in here anymore.

"Buzz." Three o'clock. My heart leaps with anticipation and excitement. School's out. Everyone hastens their goodbyes and best wishes, then rushes out of the classroom into another crowd of excited people. Everyone, that is, except me. I simply sit there, not wishing to worry about the crowds. All that is left in the quickly abandoned classroom are myself and the professor.

The professor stands, ruffling some papers into order. He looks up, task complete and addresses me.

"So, Meridal, are you ready to embark on your adventure to England?"

"Adventure?" I reply with raised eyebrows. "Funny you should put it that way, Professor Hughs. But yes, indeed I am!"

"That'll be the best place for inspiration on your thesis work. Have you decided definitively who or what will be your subject?" the professor asks.

"Oh, yes I have!" I say enthusiastically. "I am going to do my thesis project on British Folklore and Legends, that is, Robin Hood in particular." The professor smiles a knowing smile back at me.

"Ah, yes," he begins slowly, "I had thought you'd lean in that direction towards him. He has so fascinated you these past three years." He continues on to say, "You have a real flair for seeing into the stories and grasping what really goes on there."

"Thank you," I reply, slightly embarrassed by his unusual praise. "Well, the legends are so alive, even in today's world. The stories about him still influence our lives through modern films and literature. There's a lot to get excited about!"

"True." The professor chuckles then, remembering his own fire and curiosity at this age. "Well, you had better be off. The crowd seems to have dispersed. Good luck across the pond." He stops then in the doorway, looking back at me and adds, "For now and always."

"Thank you again, Professor Hughs, for your insights, wonderful classes and lectures. If it wasn't for you, I'd never have thought about the study abroad program. Goodbye," I respond. Then grabbing my books and bag, I follow him out of the classroom. He stops and locks the door as I walk away. He watches me walk away from him towards the dorms.

"God be with you, my lady," he whispers as she continues to walk farther away from him, "God be with you."

··●··

"The plane will be landing in ten minutes at Heathrow International Airport. Please return your seats to their upright positions and refasten your seatbelts. Please turn off all laptops and other electronic devices and stow them safely for landing. Thank you for flying with World International Airways. We hope your stay is a pleasant one," the flight attendant announced over the intercom system of the plane.

I have been asleep for almost eight hours for the approximate ten-hour flight. Now, I am wide awake, and ready to see my new world. While waiting to land, my thoughts drift back to my departure. The goodbyes had been more difficult than I had anticipated. My mother and father would miss me dearly. I hoped they realized how much I would miss them and how much I love them.

The plane lands with a soft bounce and pulls me from my thoughts. I can feel the pressure of the engine shifting to slow us down. I am grateful for my window seat and enjoy watching as we taxi off the runway to our gate. I was also fortunate to not have anyone in the seat next to me, which meant that getting myself together to deplane might take a bit longer. Although I am eager to get moving, I decide to let the other passengers who are near ready to stand get off first. I smile at myself as I finally admit it consciously, "I hate crowds."

So I wait.

It surprises me how quickly the plane emptied, so it really wasn't much of a wait. With my stuff all back in its proper bags, I proceed to disembark. I have just a carry-on and a garment bag until I reach baggage claim and get my big suitcase. After I balance the weight to allow for brisk walking, I exit the plane. In my head, I hear the professor's words and smile to myself, my adventure begins!

I find the baggage claim area easily and after retrieving my suitcase, I am again so grateful for my mother's smart thinking about luggage with wheels. What a game changer! Now, off to Customs to have my passport stamped. The line isn't very long and moves swiftly. Beyond all the hustling and bustling of the other travelers, I spot the cardboard sign I am looking for - OXFORD UNIVERSITY. I feel my heart racing with excitement, anticipation, and the stomach butterflies are fluttering. The sign is held by a pleasant-looking girl of my own age.

"Hi," I say brightly to her. "I am Meridal from the United States. Are you my welcoming committee?"

"Indeed I am!" she responds, smiling back at me. "I'm Corina!"

"Well, it is sure great to meet you, Corina. Where do we go from here? Are we to take a bus, or do you have a car?" I ask, realizing my bags are heavier than I wanted.

"Oh! Yes, of course. I have a car, just outside." She eyes my bags and offers to help. So between the two of us, we get my American-sized luggage into her modest-sized British car.

We chat idly during the ride about nothing of real importance. I am glad to find her so charming; she has an ease about her that makes me feel comfortable. Little did I know then that we were to become the closest of friends.

It is nightfall when we finally reach the students' resident hall. It is then that I learn Corina is to be my roommate. The apartment, or rather "flat," is larger than I expected or hoped. I am very appreciative. My things may seem small when packed, but not so much when unpacked. OOH! I did bring a dreadful amount of stuff.

As I am unpacking, I notice that Corina has many of the same books I have concerning folklore and legends. so I ask, "Corina, is your major Literature too?"

"Yes. I thought you knew that. That is why we were paired as roommates, for our similarities in our specialties. My thesis project will also be British Legends, but for myself, I would prefer the subject of King Arthur and his court," she tells me, her eyes flashing with the same sort of passion I imagine mine possess when I speak of Robin Hood.

"Wow, this is great!" I say with genuine enthusiasm, remembering that none of the kids back home ever wanted to discuss "old fairy tales."

"Tomorrow," Corina continues cheerfully, "If you feel up to it, I've arranged for us to tour Nottinghamshire. And, the day after, I've planned a trip to Salisbury and the surrounding area."

"You're not joking, are you??" I answer excitedly. "Ah, that'd be the best! To really see where Robin Hood and his merry men lived and fought the evil Sheriff! Wow, up to it??? What time do we leave?"

Corina giggles at my response, "I thought you'd feel this way about it. We should be off early in the morrow, about six a.m. or so."

"6 a.m.?" I question, causing a tiny frown upon her brow. I shrug, smile, and answer, "Well, I am very glad that I slept so much on the flight over here. 6 a.m. it is!" And with my agreement, the smile returns to her face.

I wasn't quite settled in, but my hunger has. I leave the rest of the unpacking till later and let Corina know that anytime she wanted to go out to dinner was good with me. Corina had arranged for us to meet up with some of her friends, and together we all go to a local favorite pub. The specialty there is Fish and Chips. It tastes like heaven. The talk is lively and very comfortable amidst the fantastic atmosphere and food and drink. I love listening to their accents.

By the time we return to our flat, I am quite ready to retire to my bed. I quickly change into my pajamas, say my prayer, but fall asleep before I can say "amen."

··●··

The morning mist held long and fast. Not wishing to rise, I looked around, not quite sure of my location. The trees seemed to loom above, as giant guardians, keeping me confined to this small area. I could hear noises around me, but could put no particular names to the sounds. Far off in the distance, one sound rang clear - the blow of hunting horn.

It was not the same sound associated with the commencement of the fox hunt, but similar. I looked around myself again. Surely I should recognize this area. I didn't feel threatened, only penned in. I resolved to leave. I headed in the direction I faced since I didn't feel any other direction had greater importance than any other.

As I began to move, I felt a sickening spinning sensation, then...blackness.

··●··

I wake to the sound of my alarm clock buzzing. The clock reads 5 a.m. I look around my room, half-suspecting I am in a forest. What a dream! I sit up slowly and stretch. I am sitting in my room in a student's flat in Oxford. I pull my legs up and into me, still under the covers, and smile. "What a dream, indeed," I say to myself. Then, swinging my legs off the side of the bed, resting my feet on the cold floor, I realize I have yet to unpack my slippers.

I can hear Corina in the kitchen, and I can smell the coffee brewing. Not wanting to take the time to find my slippers, I reach for a pair of thick socks on top of my open suitcase and pull them on. Upon standing, I straighten my pajamas and pull a sweater over them, and I am ready for my coffee and good mornings.

My mind is still full of the dream. I guess I had it because of my excitement about our trip today. Imagine...Nottingham! Sherwood Forest! Corina didn't notice my mental distraction, as she sluggishly moves about the kitchen. She greets me with a yawn, then a sleepy smile, and then an important question.

"Would you like to take the first shower? I'd feel dreadful if your first shower here was to be a cold one. Besides, it'll take a cold shower to wake me up today. I do believe that Bitter from last night is still battering my brain this morning." She winces and moves her hand to steady her head.

"You'd better be careful," I tease. "You still look a little pissed (the new word I learned for drunk) to me." She sighs in agreement and makes her way across the kitchen to the coffee maker. I do an about-face and head back into my room to grab what I need for my shower.

After both of us have showered and dressed, we sit down together for a proper, though brief, breakfast. Corina suggests that we leave the dishes for later, no complaints from me. We both head off into our rooms to gather what we want to have for the day's trip. I grab my camera, notebook and a light parka jacket to serve as both a windbreaker and a raincoat. I rejoin Corina in the main room where she has not only her own gear but also an extra basket that contains snack food for our day. We lock the flat and off we go!

The streets are surprisingly busy at this early hour. Corina points out that tea time is 4 o'clock in the afternoon, and that most people prefer it as the end of the workday rather than as a break.

It is about 100 miles on the M1 and allowing for a much higher speed limit than in the USA, the estimated travel time is just two hours and a bit. The countryside that we drive through absolutely enchants me. As the sky grows lighter and brighter, the greenery around us shimmers with the dew.

We reach West Bridgeford at about 8:30 a.m., and I can no longer resist the urge to take photos of the beauty I see in England. West Bridgeford is the Administrative Center of Nottinghamshire. We refuel the car with "petrol". It will take us another 30 minutes or so to reach the City of Nottingham.

As we drive into the city, I...well, breathtaking is too insignificant a word. Corina smiles at my reaction. She has a lot of pride in her country, and it shows. I admire that in her. I have to pinch myself to make sure I am not dreaming, because there it is, in front of my eyes, just as it has always stood in my mind's eye, Nottingham Castle.

We park the car near the old castle. Corina takes some bread and cheese from the basket and puts them into her daypack. I guess my look has a question in it, because she responds, "Exploring always makes me hungry. You'll see." And she winks at me knowingly.

"Oh, I'll never argue about the necessity of food." I laugh with her, knowing that exploring always makes me hungry too.

At my first glance of the castle, I have a deja vu sort of feeling, which passes quickly and I chalk it up to all the years of reading and studying and seeing movies of and about the characters and stories from this place. But as we approach the castle, and stand before the great gates, the deja vu feeling becomes overwhelming. I pause in my steps, and shake my head to clear it. Corina stops and turns to me with concern in her eyes. She puts her hand on my shoulder and asks, "Are you okay?"

"Yes, yes. I'm fine, probably a little jet lag catching up with me," I answer. Then I ask, "Can we go inside?"

"Oh yes, of course!" Corina reassures me. "I wouldn't have brought you all this way to stand outside and imagine what it must be like in here. If you're ready now, you'll need to show your student I.D."

I smile back at her, "Oh, I'm ready. And I've already got it out!"

Passing through the high gates, into the courtyard, I can see the tournament field where Robin had split the arrow, thus winning the contest and Maid Marian's heart. Standing there and looking out over the field, I can visualize the entire scene...almost as if it were actually happening. I can hear the cheering, and smell the smells of the day. I can see Robin taking his last shot of the contest, hear the cheers that arose, see the anger on the Sheriff's face as Robin is awarded the prize instead of the Sheriff's contestant, and I can see the spark of new love on Marian's face as Robin hands over the prize he has been awarded to her; His first gift to her, a small golden arrow. I feel a hand on my shoulder. It is Corina gently urging me on. And just as fast as the scene had appeared, it was gone.

"Hey, Meridal, there is much more to see than this dusty and overgrown field. Come on, don't you want to go inside?" she asks, with just a tinge of concern in her voice.

"Right. Yes. It's just all so beautiful," I say, knowing my voice has a faraway sound to it.

"Well," Corina continues, "If an old field can dazzle you like this, you better get a hold of yourself for the magic inside the castle." And with that, Corina grabs my hand and, with a light laugh, leads me inside.

The temperature inside the castle is much cooler than the outside temperature. I gasp when we enter the main hall. Corina says I'll get used to the temperature soon enough, mistaking the reason for my gasp. A chilling sense of recognition has washed over me as we enter into the castle. It must be all of the excitement, I tell myself, but...I know it is more than that. For right now, I'm going to ignore it and analyze later.

The smell of the castle is somewhat dank. You can feel the age of the place. "Wow," I sigh aloud. Corina only giggles at my reaction.

"Yeah, I know," she says.

We walk from room to room, and then returning to the main gathering hall, we sit for a while. Corina asks if I want to see the dungeons below, and I shake my head 'no.' As we were passing through the rooms before, I notice that one room in particular seems more welcoming than the others. The room is sparsely decorated with only a great canopied bed and a full standing mirror. The room seems bright and cheery for all its lack of personal items. I have a feeling it must be the room Marian had stayed in during her time in the castle. So I ask Corina about it. Her response surprises me.

"Wow, you really did your background work on the personalities for your research. That is, or was, the room that Marian stayed in. It wasn't posted anywhere. How did you know that?" Corina asks.

"Well," I stumble a bit on my answer, "because I guess if I had lived here, that would be the room I would want." And my answer is both true and a lie. I knew it was Marian's room...but how?

Corina seems satisfied with my answer, and then says to me, "Well, I'm gonna go check out the dungeons."

"Ok," I answer. "I think I'll loop back through the rooms again."

"Great," Corina says, "meet back here in thirty minutes?" I smile back at her and nod in agreement.

I, of course, head straight back up to Marian's bedroom. I want to linger with my thoughts. There weren't a lot of restrictions in the castle, so I go over and sit on the bed. I imagine what it must have been like for Marian to live here, once upon a time. I notice a ray of sun beginning to shine into the room through an open window. It reflects upon the mirror and then catches upon something on the floor. After getting off the bed and walking a few steps, I bend down to inspect the sparkle closer.

I catch my breath. How could this be? For there, lying on the floor in front of me is a tiny golden arrow not unlike the one that Robin had won and then gave as a gift to Marian on that fateful tournament day. Not believing it could actually be real, I reach out to touch it. As my fingers grasp the small golden arrow, the sunbeam fades. I am surprised by the sudden withdrawal of light. Almost afraid to open my hand, I do anyway, and there, laying upon my open palm is a golden arrow. Marian's arrow! The detail on the arrow is simply stunning. There is the point of the arrow, then four intricately carved golden roses, and then finally the tail feathers of the arrow. I look around myself quickly, knowing this can't be happening, but instinctively I quickly hide it within my coat pocket...such a treasure, I will not part with it.

I stand up, and trying not to look suspicious or guilty, I make my way out of the room and down to the lower areas to rejoin Corina. I have already made up my mind not to share this treasure with anyone.

When we finally leave the castle, it is noon. I am so hungry, and very thankful that Corina had the forethought to bring food. We start out for Sherwood Forest after our brief lunch. We cross the infamous footbridge where Robin Hood had met Little John for the first time. We walk all the way around the castle using the footpaths. It all feels so hauntingly familiar! The big, ageless, looming trees keeping their silent vigil. A light breeze has picked up and now rustles through their branches. To me, it seems there are whispers riding in the breeze.

The whole day, I have had startling recollections of familiarity. I keep them to myself. Corina and I are having a very good time together sharing this day. By about 4 p.m., tea time, we make our way into a nearby inn for some stew and brew, and then dessert and tea! We have worked up a good appetite. I am very grateful for the warm food and savory dessert.

We return to our car a bit after 5 p.m., and I am so grateful I am not driving. I feel completely exhausted, and I fall asleep on the ride home as soon as we leave Nottingham city limits.

··●··

I was in the forest again. The mist had risen, leaving the place less foreboding. The horn still sounded occasionally in the distance. I was moving now, outside of the original glen where I had awakened. The sound of the horn seemed to become closer with each step forward I took. Was I to meet someone? I couldn't recall.

I could now hear a new sound floating through the trees. The glorious sound of a harp joyfully played. Men's voices rose and fell in rhythm with the tune. I was in Sherwood! Hadn't I just left? I must be headed towards the outlaw's camp. Would they see me?? I hoped not. Still I moved on, faster and faster. It seemed my steps kept time to the quickening rhythm of the tune. The music reached a sort of hysteria, the forest around me became a blur. Abruptly the music stopped, and my forward motion with it.

I looked around to see where I had come. I stood outside a ring, or screen, of shrubbery. I looked along the ring for an inconspicuous vantage point to peer through. What a sight to behold! I had goosebumps everywhere. Through the shrubbery on the inside of the ring, was Robin Hood, and all of his closest men. They were engaged in lively conversation. I drew in my breath in surprise, quickly covering my mouth with my hand lest I betray myself to them.

As I got a hold of myself, I relaxed my hand, resting it on my throat. I kept my hand upon my throat in surprise of what I felt under my hand. Using my fingers to explore the detail of what I felt there, I knew it could be nothing else but the golden arrow fastened to my collar. It was then that I noticed my attire. I was dressed much the same as the men I viewed inside the shrubbery. I wore a green suede long-sleeved jerkin, a green suede split riding skirt, and green suede knee boots with a dagger attached to the left boot top. Around my waist hung a small sword. Was I an active participant or observer here? Is this a dream??

My question was immediately answered, as I involuntarily pushed through the shrubbery screen into the men's full view. All turned to welcome me. One man, distinguishably handsome, obviously Robin Hood, moved towards me with a familiarity and a smile.

"Marian, you've returned," he said while reaching out to me.

··●··

"Meridal, Meridal. Wake up. We're home," says the familiar voice of Corina.

"Huh?" is all I can muster to say in return. I am so dazed.

"Wake up silly. You're a bit big for me to be carrying you. You slept the whole way back, boy, you really are exhausted," Corina says. I am so disoriented. I shake my head, trying to rattle my thoughts back into place. Back into the here and now.

"Wow, what a dream!" I answer sleepily as we walk up the stairs to our flat front door. "I dreamt that I was in Sherwood with Robin Hood, and that I was Marian!" I confess to her.

"Oh, really?" says Corina in a teasing manner. I realize I just handed her loads of ammo for social embarrassment. But then she shows her truer colors. "Well, my lady," she starts again, friendly, draping her arm over my shoulders, "that can happen when you go traipsing around these old haunts." She giggles and unlocks our door. She's trying to be serious and then tells me, "You better stay close to me when we're at Stonehenge, don't want you falling through some doorway in time, do we now?" I have to laugh with her. The silly fancies of a romantic student, that's all today has been. And I put my hand to my pocket, but didn't I have the arrow to prove that it is more?

As we enter our flat, I head straight towards my room. Corina laughs at how tired I appear. I am content to have her believe that. I need time to be alone and think. As I close my door, she yells, "Hey, what about the dishes?"

"Tomorrow," I call back to her. "Tomorrow." And with that I close my door and quietly lock it, making sure it is secure.

I reach into my pocket and pull forth the little treasure, my golden arrow. I muse over that thought, 'my golden arrow', but I somehow know it has been left there for me to find. Didn't that make it mine? The arrow still feels warm in my hand, like when I first picked it up inside that sunbeam.

I turn the arrow over and over in my hands, wondering how it had been there at the castle on the very day I was. Also, I wonder how it had been fastened to my collar while in my forest dream. I can see no way to pin it on. But in my further examination, I pricked my finger, so learning the secret. What a treasure indeed! The excitement I feel inside reminds me of champagne bubbles.

Dare I wear it? I throw off my jacket and go to the mirror and hold it up to my collar. Then, I shift my eyes up and look at myself, my face, in the mirror. And another question comes to mind, how could Robin and his men have mistaken me for their beloved Marian? I mean, weren't they all close? Didn't they live in close quarters? How could I, a stranger, be mistaken for her?

And, as I ask myself these questions, while looking into the mirror, the mirror image ripples. I blink and steady myself by grabbing onto the bureau in front of me where the mirror rests. I think to myself that I must be much more tired than I think I am. After steadying myself, I look again at my reflection in the mirror. The mirror ripples again, but this time I don't sway; I am transfixed. Slowly, the room in the reflection behind me transforms into a forest scene. Sherwood! I can see a gathering of people celebrating something. I strain my eyes to look deeper and see better. There stood two figures set apart from the crowd. It seems a moonbeam rests on them, giving them a magical and shimmery kinda glow. This is a marriage celebration! A shiver runs through me, and I can feel the gooseflesh on my arms. I know this day, and I know the two standing apart and together. This is the wedding of Robin and Marian!

I strain my eyes to look even closer, but I think I know in my heart what my eyes would see. Maybe because I want this to be true. As Robin lifts the veil from the face of his bride to share a marriage kiss, I see clearly her face, Marian's face - MY face!

I blink my eyes while taking in a large and loud sigh. And then I find myself once more in my room, in my flat in Oxford, in my present time. Using my hand to try and feel for a chair to sit down on, I miss and thump down on the floor.

Then, there's a knock on my door.

"Meridal, are you okay? It sounded like something fell," Corina asked.

Knowing if I didn't respond convincingly, I will worry her, I answer, "Yes, silly me, I tripped while taking my pants off."

"Ok, well, obviously you're tired, but don't you think you should eat some supper?" Corina asks, obviously concerned about my odd behavior.

"You know Corina," I answer, "I will come out and eat with you, and then I'll do the dishes as well." And with that I can hear Corina leaving my door and returning to the kitchen.

First, this arrow needs to go into my jewelry box for safekeeping. Second, I need to quickly change my clothes to cover my story. And, third, I need some time away from this mystery so I can relax about being crazy.

We both wake early the next morning. We are both eager to get started. Although I am still preoccupied with my thoughts about everything that happened yesterday, dinner and a good night's sleep last night helped to make me feel more confident in my reality of the here and now. In an attempt to not make my new roommate and friend worry needlessly, I had prepared breakfast for the two of us today, and had done the dishes along the way, so clean up is easy. After finishing breakfast, I ask if Corina wants me to pack us a lunch.

"No need to pack a lunch today," she answers. "There is a great restaurant in Salisbury where we have a booking, best Fish and Chips and Shepherd's Pie anywhere!"

"Okay, well that will be better than anything I could whip up to pack!" I answer enthusiastically. I really love Fish and Chips.

"But just in case our breakfast wears off on the ride there, let's stop off at the pastry shop and grab a scone and some coffee for the ride," Corina adds.

I smile, responding, "Corina, I like the way you think."

The drive to Salisbury, where the legendary Stonehenge stands, is approximately 70 miles away, a one and a half hour drive. Again, I am enchanted by the countryside we drive through. Realizing

I've been exceptionally quiet during the drive, I speak my thoughts out loud, "The countryside is so beautiful."

"Yes, it is," she responds. "You know growing up here, and seeing it all the time, it can become just part of the background. It is refreshing to see it through your eyes. It brings back the magic quality to it all. And speaking of magic, Stonehenge is loaded with it. For as much as it has been studied by modern man, it is still such a mystery!"

Sensing Corina is in the mood for conversation, I cheerfully respond, "Some scientists believe it to be a large calendar, a huge sundial of sorts, capable of predicting eclipses and other such phenomena. While other people, from a diverse range of studies, tell that it is some kind of temple for worshipping the moon."

Corina smiles as she continues to drive safely along, and adds, "Yes, some people swear it has magical powers. Some myths tell that the ancient kings and the druidic class fancied it as a time and space portal. I don't know which I believe, but whichever it is, it is magnificent!"

My curiosity is sparked now. "Isn't Stonehenge connected to the Summer Solstice?" I ask.

"Yes," answered Corina, "that is the biggest visiting day here for tourists, scientists and pagan worshippers. There is a stone marker which has been set to cast a shadow upon the altar during the Summer Solstice, which is today, June 21st."

"Oh my goodness! I have lost all track of the date." I turn to look at her slyly, "You're pretty sneaky, aren't you?"

"Well..." she looks sheepishly at me, "who knew I'd be able to surprise you with something like this!"

I look out the window, it was still dark, but I knew that night was turning into day. "Will we make it before sunrise?" I ask anxiously.

"Look up ahead of us," she says. And as I look out the window, my eyes get their first glimpse of Stonehenge, and I have goosebumps everywhere. "Aaah," escapes from my mouth, as my hand moves up to my heart, as I see the awesomeness of this place.

Corina lets me know that we will have to walk a bit because they don't let the cars get too close anymore. But it is not too long of a walk. She pulls into the car park, the attendant checks our parking permit, and then directs us to our spot. Both of us are very eager to get out of the car and start moving toward the monument.

As we get closer, the size and scope of the site become clearer. It is the most beautiful and most ancient place I have ever seen. To have been built so long ago, before modern technologies, for a purpose that even today no one is sure about or understands, has me speechless. We are about to participate in something that has been observed for thousands of years...it is like looking through a door that opens into the past.

There is already quite a crowd, but we expected that, and Corina seems to know exactly where we should go to get the best effect. I eagerly follow her as she weaves through the crowd. We have just come to a spot and stopped as a collective pause falls on the crowd. The air feels tingly with anticipation. It feels like magic being born.

Corina has worked us through the crowd so that we are standing very close to the altar stone where the shadow should fall. The light is rising with the sun. As the sun continues to rise, the shadow upon the land continues stretching toward the altar stone. With my camera ready, I whisper to Corina, "I have got to get a picture of this," and then I step into the shadow to take my shot. The air feels cooler...unnaturally so. I ignore it though because I don't want to miss the moment. The shadow reaches the altar stone, and then I am nowhere and everywhere.

I feel like I am outside looking in on the space where I can see myself standing, and Corina. I didn't feel like I could move anything but my eyes. My eyes focus on the altar, and then all of me moves in the shadow to the altar where I watch myself lay my hands upon the stone. I can hear Corina screaming in the background, but she is so far away

The air is not only tingly but icy cold, but I am not shivering nor am I cold. I feel warmed by something. I find I can move my hands, and I reach up to touch the arrow pin I had put on this morning. The pin is hot, and its heat is increasing, almost a searing heat. I feel myself screaming at the pain of the burn, but I cannot hear my voice. The world had no up or down, and I know what is coming next—the blackness of passing out.

Voices? Yes, I can hear voices. Far off and frantic, all mixed up.

"Meridal!"

"Marian!"

Names, different, yet the same. Two, but one.

I can feel my body again. I can breathe, although the air I inhale has a strangeness to it that I cannot name.

I feel heavy. I want to open my eyes. I want to open my eyes. I want to open my eyes, and it seems such a struggle. So, I decide to try moving instead, fingers, and arms... "AUUGH," I gasp from the pain, but it helps me to open my eyes, only to see a very unfamiliar face watching me. Unfamiliar and familiar...this person looks like Friar Tuck. I must be in a dream. But the pain I am feeling goes far beyond any dream I have ever experienced.

The man's face held such concern for me, "Easy little flower. What is it you need?" he asks me. What do I need?? I think to myself, how about some clarity on the situation! I decide on civility since obviously I am in need of his help.

"Where am I?" I ask. What a stupid question, but I asked it anyway.

"Safe with us in Sherwood of course," he answers with such satisfaction.

"Sherwood??" I ask confused, "I was at Stonehenge."

"Yes, yes," he assures me, "but now you're here and safe. You just lay back and rest. You're not quite healed from the arrow wound." He says it so matter-of-factly, like I get shot every day!

"Arrow wound? How did I get shot by an arrow?" I wish I didn't sound so pathetic as I ask this.

"The Sheriff's men caught us passing through Stonehenge as we paid tribute this morning, and, well, I'm not sure how it all happened in the confusion," Tuck tries to explain to me.

Not being able to leave well enough alone, I ask one more question that is sure to raise his guard. "Who do you think I am?" I ask anyway. I'm pretty sure I know the answer he'll give. And, of course this question gives him great pause.

"Marian? Marian, are you okay? I mean did you hit your head or something when you fell?" Tuck asks with a great deal of concern upon his face.

"Yes, Tuck, I am fine," I lie, "just a bit confused by all of it. I'll be fine. You always do such a good job with your care of others and wound dressing." The fact that I use his name calms him down. Me, though, I am anything but calm. I am lying here, in Sherwood, with an arrow wound, and known to all who see me as Marian of Sherwood, the bride of Robin Hood.

This isn't a dream; somehow, I am here for real. Reading and researching about a subject and then stepping into their world is a bit more than I am ready for. It has something to do with my arrow pin, Marian's arrow...and of course Stonehenge. Well, I could certainly let all the experts and scientists know what it's all about now, and as soon as I tell them, they'll lock me up in a sanitarium.

I lay my head back down on my pillow on my makeshift bed in a hut in Sherwood Forest, knowing fully well that if I fall asleep, I will awaken once more here. Tuck is still muttering to himself as he moves about seeing to the camp. I give in to my tiredness and fall asleep.

It is a fitful sleep, and I wake easily, as my ears can hear that there is movement around me. I want to seem as if I am still asleep, but the pain from my wound causes me to both wince and cry out a bit. A man rushed again to my bedside. I expect to see Tuck's face, but I don't. I see the face I have dreamt about my whole life... and most recently in the car ride with Corina, Robin Hood's face. There are trails of tears under his eyes, strained with worry. It is very obvious to me that he hasn't been sleeping.

"Marian," is all he could manage to say without his eyes over-welling. His eyes...oh, I think my heart stopped a bit when I looked into them. His eyes hold such depths of love for me. So kind and gentle a man, he had been named an outlaw throughout history, at this moment, I could not see why. He lightly touches my face, and I can feel myself leaning into his hand. I close my eyes and then fly them open as I feel his lips touch my own. He pulls back from me, and has a question in his eyes now.

Just then, Tuck re-entered into the little room; he coughs to announce his arrival. Robin sits back, still with a guarded look on his face. "Yes?" he asks Tuck as he looks towards him. Tuck coughs into his hand, then clears his throat, obviously whatever he wants to tell Robin he doesn't want me to hear. Robin sighs, then turns back to me. "We'll talk later after you're better rested."

And I only nod in response. I watch the two men leave the room, and although I want to do anything but sleep, my body wins and sleep it is.

When I re-awaken, it seems darker than before in the hut or room. I feel much more alert and myself now, and as I look around where I am, I realize I am in a makeshift room inside of a cave. I can sense the dankness now. I am also more able to move around without such searing pain. Sigh, ok...I need to think. I touch the clothing around my neck. The clothing feels unfamiliar. I sit up and throw the blankets off to see that I am wearing a roughly made nightdress. And no arrow. A kind of slow panic starts to arise in my stomach. I need that arrow. Somehow that arrow is a portal key, and I know I need it to get back to my home.

The light is very low in the room, and I am trying to be very quiet. At the moment I am alone, but I don't want to risk being caught searching around. What I most wanted to find, besides the arrow, is my clothing. But it is only the clothing that I do find, the green suede outfit from my "dream." It is laid out upon a stout stool with great care. I check the collar of the jerkin to see if the arrow is there, but no luck. Maybe it has fallen off. So I quietly bend down and with my hands acting as my eyes, I search in the hay that is used as floor covering. Then, all of a sudden I am not alone. I freeze and try to breathe. I could sense there is someone standing behind me, and since they didn't announce they are there, I don't know what to do. But I know I can't stay crouching there on the floor, so I stand and turn to face whoever it is. They are standing in the darkness of the doorway, and I put all the courage I can into my voice, "Who's there?"

"Don't you know me, Meridal?" he asks quietly in return, still keeping to the shadows. His voice has an edge to it that urges caution and truth telling. I simply stand there, not knowing what truth to tell. He steps into what there is of light in the room and holds out an open hand, palm up with a golden arrow. The arrow! My arrow!

I look from his hand to his face, and meet his eyes, and ask my own question in response, "Yes, I know you, Robin Hood. More importantly, I think the question is, how do you know me? I am not of your time."

He ignores my question and asks another, "You are the proper owner of this, are you not?" He raises his hand a little higher to indicate the treasure laying there in his palm.

"I believe that I am," I answer, but I still feel cautious and a bit unsure.

47

"Then, this is how I know you. You may call yourself a different name, but you are, and always have been, my love Marian," he answers.

"I don't understand what's happening here," I say, bringing both hands up to my head to run my hands back through my hair, as if by brushing it back, I could see more clearly. All I do is realize anew the pain of my injury, which causes me to gasp and stumble a bit. Robin moves to steady me, and I put my hand up in defiance and move to sit upon the bed.

My obvious discomfort softens his voice and energy, and he lowers his body to a squatting position so we are more level in the room. And then he continues, "Time is all relevant. Every plane is connected in the same space but at different levels. Marian was wounded, almost dead, here. While at the same time, on another plane, your time, you live. But you and her are one and the same, and your strength has been needed here. Marian called and you, Meridal, answered. You called yourself back here. You called yourself because I can't bear a life without you." And with that answer out in the open, Robin sits down hard on the floor, shoulders slumped and head bowed.

As I sit on the bed, looking at this broken man, I am literally beside myself! How dare I pull myself from one life back into another. What a headache I have. I am so angry, and feel so used, and, and....I don't even know what else. Breathe. I need to breathe. I look again at this man, this man I so love that I pulled myself back through time to save his love. And then I think about why I have felt so passionate about his legend and his life and his world, and I can totally understand why I am sitting here in this cave on this bed at this moment.

But I also know I cannot stay here. I know that the arrow is my key. As he sits there, vulnerable and unguarded, I see the arrow in his palm.

"Robin," I say his name softly, and he raises his eyes to mine. He shifts his body to be closer to me, the arrow is there, and before he closes his hand around it, I snatch it into my own. His eyes turn frantic as he knows what will come next, and I can hear his voice trail off as I hold the arrow to my heart and cold blackness enfolds me.

In that cold flash, I am back at Stonehenge with Corina. I am laying on the damp ground and looking straight up into the worried face of my friend.

"Are you okay?" she asks anxiously. "You just sort of fainted all of a sudden."

Sitting myself up, and dusting off the grass and bits of ground, I answer, "Oh yes, Corina. I'm just fine," I say, smiling weakly. There is a crowd of looky-loos but now that I am sitting, they lose interest and begin to move about. I look at her face again, and smile with a bit more strength and ask, "You don't have any more field trips scheduled for us, do you?"

She laughs, relieved, "No, I think we're good for now." That said, she reaches out and hugs me. When she releases me, I ask my own question, "Corina, you wouldn't be hungry now, would you?"

··●··

My school year is coming to a close. I never did return to The United States. I guess I could say that the English countryside is just too agreeable...but in my heart, I know I felt closer to love here. What an incredible year it has been. Corina and I never discussed that day at Stonehenge any more deeply than I was overrun with travel exhaustion. I, though, think about that day every day and wonder, what if I had stayed? I wear my arrow every day. I have never forgotten what Robin taught me about time. I know his Marian died, and I feel a sadness for Robin and his men and I wonder how they are faring. I had read the available research, and fulfilled all my study requirements and written a brilliant paper, but the truth of what I wrote about and what I know always nags at me.

I am booked for a trip back to the States to see my family before returning here to England for a postgraduate career. It is June again, and I feel a bit prickly and anxious, knowing what the past June had shown me. I am excited for my trip home, and I am busy packing what I will need for a short trip when the phone rings. It's the long-distance call no one ever wants to receive. My parents had been in a terrible car crash. I have been crying for three days. I don't even remember the details, just the reality and the loss. Corina does her best to help me through it...but this type of loss...teaches me something different. It reminds me that love is forever, and that I can believe my parents are happy and alive together on another plane in time. I can also now understand why Marian pulled me to her time. There is no more thinking, I know what to do.

Early on June 21st, one year later, I hail myself a taxi out to Stonehenge for the coming Solstice. I leave before Corina is awake, and I leave a note telling her I've gone home and for her not to worry. I know she will...but I hope for not too long. I have only a very small bag of my most precious items. The taxi makes good time and once we arrive, I pay him and thank him. The crowd this year is smaller, so it is easier to position myself exactly where I want to be.

I am filled with anticipation and hope. There is no guarantee what kind of reaction I will receive when I get there. I am trusting in love. The dawning begins. The shadow begins its stretch toward the altar stone and at the moment it is to touch the stone, I step purposefully into the shadow. The darkness and cold I feel are welcomed, and this time, there is no burning pain in my chest. Instead, I feel tingly all over, and I can hear voices, laughter and singing swirling around me. Then, as suddenly as it started, it all goes still.

I blink my eyes to refocus my sight, and I see that I am standing in a misty forest. I am dressed in green suede, with my travel bag slung over my shoulder. I instinctively reach toward my throat to where my arrow pin should be, and I sigh and relax, it is there. And I am here.

I am startled by the sound of a hunting horn calling in the forest. I listen to the direction it is strongest and then head off in an easy trot towards the sound. I guess I am not as alert as I had hoped because I run headlong into an ambush of men in forester's attire similar to mine. They stare at me in dumb-faced silence. One amongst them moves forward towards me. He is hooded, dressed the same as the other men. He stops in front of me and then lets his hood fall. He seemed older to me, yet his eyes are still those I know.

He searches my face, waiting for an explanation. Oh boy, not good at on-the-spot speeches, I simply announce, "I've returned to you here, and now, of my own free will. I have nothing left for me in my now, save wonderful memories. Here, there is a living purpose and a sense of belonging. You and your words have never left me." I realize I am shaking when he takes my hand into his and lifts it to his lips for a gentle kiss. And then he bows and says, "Welcome is your return, Lady Meridal." He addresses me by my modern name, which causes me to smile and tear up.

"You may call me by my first name, Marian," I reply.

"So be it." He then bends down on one knee, taking my hand into his. His eyes lift to meet mine with a stare that holds so many things. A smile gently crosses my lips. Here I am home. I gently pull Robin up from his kneeling position, and, taking my hand from his, place both of my hands on his shoulders. I pull him close and kiss him squarely on the lips. He is surprised, as are his men, but he answers my kiss in kind.

As if just realizing we are not alone, we break apart to look at each other, both of us are smiling, and Robin raises one eyebrow. I answer the expression on his face with, "I am a modern girl at heart, expect no less from me than to be me, dear heart." His men burst into laughter and gather around us, all welcoming me home. A joyful song rings out as we make our way back to the home camp.

A smile plays upon my lips as I walk, holding hands with Robin Hood through the forest. There is no regret, just hope and love.

And so the life of Meridal ends and begins anew as Marian, the Lady of Sherwood.

...and they live happily ever after.

··●··

As the dream faded, Forbes realized he was not in the same place he had been when the dream-sleep came upon him. He was back in his guest sleeping hut. He also sensed he was not alone. It took him a minute or two to remember that he had been at breakfast after a storytelling event and had met a stranger named Greer.

CHAPTER 2

So Many Questions and the Long Walk

The sky had already darkened. The youth had come to check on the storyteller, only to find him still asleep while Greer stayed hidden in the dark shadows within the hut. The youth left once more, but Greer knew he would be back. She had learned that the hospitality of a storyteller was of great importance, and if the youth had been neglectful in his duties and some harm had befallen the storyteller while he was here, there would be dire consequences for the youth. Greer knew she must leave for her own safety, but she needed to talk to this man more. Carter had taught her well the safety of being outside. Just being in this hut made her feel trapped and afraid. She wasn't sure why she had been drawn to listen to this storyteller. She supposed it was that she missed her father and craved company other than her cow, Jow's. She also knew she needed to learn more of this world in order to find her place in it, her purpose. But how could this man know her life?? *How did he know?* She kept asking herself in her mind. There was no reasonable answer she could come up with. So, she found herself confronting this man, and then he fainted?! She was so frustrated. She didn't enjoy feeling frustrated.

As she sat there in the darkened hut watching the man twitch this way and that while he slept, she wondered and wondered and wondered. She missed her dung-smoke fire and her cow. She missed the night sky. She missed her father. She sighed. She leaned forward and rested her head face-first into her hands, which were supported by her elbows on her knees as she sat there in the dark. She wanted to cry, but she couldn't cry. She wouldn't cry. So instead she sighed again out loud once more and then straightened back up, putting her hands on her knees.

She had an odd sense of fear, the hairs on the back of her neck raised up and in front of her now sat a wide-awake storyteller. And he was watching her. In the darkened hut, she could not make out his facial expressions, and she felt her fight-or-flight kick in, but which would be the better option? His whispered question caught her off guard.

"So, you're what a woman looks like?" he asked in an incredulous voice.

"What?" she responded, incredulous herself.

"Why are you here?" he asked.

"I'm not anymore." And she rose to leave.

The storyteller panicked and said, "No, please don't go!"

She paused at the doorway. There was so much she needed to know and ask him. But flight had won the battle. Realizing she would not stay, the storyteller said, "Wait, I'll travel with you. My obligation here is over."

All she answered was, "Hurry."

The storyteller didn't have much to carry since most of whatever he needed was provided to him by the communities where he stayed. He dressed in warm layers, pulled on his boots and picked up his small black leather backpack in which he carried his personal treasures. And he knew when he looked inside next, he would find a small golden arrow. He never understood where his story-trinkets came from or why, but he knew it would be there waiting for him.

As the two made their way silently out of the community camp, Greer could see a small band of men heading down to the hut that they had just left behind. They were being led by the youth who didn't want to be held responsible for an ill storyteller. She hoped whatever penalty there would be for the youth would not be too great. The storyteller sensed her apprehension and quickened his pace to match hers. He would not be able to explain to others how he knew this story of hers if he hadn't been complicit since the beginning, which meant the same fate the Carter had feared would also be his if they were discovered together now.

After what he supposed was about two miles, he followed Greer into a screen of shrubbery. And there was the cart and cow. Obviously too big to fit into his small backpack...in fact of all the stories he had told, hers was the only one that hadn't left an item seemingly by magic in his pack. He was beginning to see why, but he still didn't understand. If he had questions, he couldn't even begin to imagine the questions she must have. He looked over at her and watched as she lovingly greeted the cow, which seemed to greet her back in the same way. His head still felt like it was swimming.

Greer looked over at him as she was checking to make sure the harness was securely attached to the cart and comfortably fitted onto the cow, and asked, "What do they call you?" Greer had learned from her Father that names held meaning. She hoped his name would give her some clues to his role in her story.

Caught a little off-guard by the sound of her voice after so much silence, he answered, "My name is Forbes Kaylynn," to which she gave no response other than a HMMPH, and kept working quietly and efficiently, moving the cart out of its protective screen.

He surmised she had come by her skills out of necessity and self-preservation. But in truth, he already knew this about her. He knew almost everything about her, and yet he realized that telling a story of someone is not the same as 'knowing' a person. Still, he was amazed by her knowledge of animal husbandry, and carting and living on her own...he had lived a very different kind of life.

Greer looked at the cow and asked, "Ready?" and to his great surprise, the cow nodded back an affirmative response. Then Greer turned to him and asked, "Ready?"

Dumbfounded by all of it unfolding before him, he, like the cow, nodded his response as to his readiness. To his surprise, Greer rolled her eyes and smiled. "Come on then, we have a very long walk before we can rest and talk."

In that brief exchange, Forbes understood the power of captivation Greer had had upon Carter. Her smile was as bright as a thousand suns, even if it was covered by months of dirt and muck and the smell of dung smoke. He willingly fell into step with Greer, the cow and the cart, no sound between them but that of their footsteps and the turn of the cartwheels. And even those sounds seemed dulled by the gathering of the misty fog that seemed to come out of nowhere.

CHAPTER 3

Making Camp, Finally

Forbes had believed he was in sturdy shape, able to endure physical activity, but this was almost more than he had strength for. She never stopped. In order not to think upon how tired his legs were, and because the rhythmic sounds of their footfalls and the turning cartwheels was somehow lulling, the storyteller allowed his thoughts to drift about in his head.

He wondered about his talents. He wondered where his stories came from. He wondered why, in a world where men were the only community he knew, he told stories of love between men and women. Why? And, then, why would his stories be so popular and welcomed if women were not? And what about the places he visited in his dreams - could they be real? The stories had always seemed so "far out" from his normal that he had never questioned if they were real. But, wasn't he walking behind a real person now? Up until a few hours ago, she was a character in a story. And what about all the items, his story-trinkets, that showed up in his backpack?

"How can this be?" he asked aloud the questions he had been asking himself. So lost was he in his own thoughts that he didn't realize the cart had stopped. So he walked right into the back of it. He made a grunting sound in reaction to the surprise and pain. And when he looked up, he saw a very scowling expression greeting him from his guide and traveling companion.

Now it was his turn to ask her, "What?" To which she simply shook her head, turned away from him and returned to walking.

Knocked, literally, out of his internal thoughts, he noticed how far they had travelled and that the light of day was beginning to change into that of nightfall. She must have sensed his next question because she looked over her shoulder and quietly said, "We'll be stopping soon."

The storyteller just smiled to himself. What a remarkable thing this all was.

Greer was true to her words, and they did stop soon. She had found another shrub to put the cart and cow behind, which offered protection from the road. Although he himself had travelled quite a bit from town to communities, he didn't recognize where they had travelled. He was quite certain he was upon a road almost no one ever travelled. It seemed that what he knew about her from her story was true; she kept to herself.

He would have offered to help her set up camp, but she seemed to move around him like he wasn't really there. And he stood there just watching with fascination at the efficiency of her movements. In no time at all, she had a ringed fire pit set up, a tarp pulled out from the cart and staked like a tent, a bag of oats and a pail of water for the cow whom she called Jow, and makeshift cushions for their seats. All they needed now was a fire. She proceeded to move to the back of the cart, again almost as in unison with his thoughts, and pulled out a burlap bag, in which she seemed to be looking for something specific. When she had found it, she brought it over and placed it inside the fire ring. Then pulling from her pocket, flint and a striker, ignited a flame. And as the smoke began, he coughed.

"Oh, that smell? Are you kidding me?" He gasped out, holding his nose. Greer turned and looked at him with the strangest expression on her face.

"Are you kidding me?" she responded in kind. "You told my whole story at that last community gathering, you've been walking behind me for miles, and now you are surprised I have lit a dung fire?" She stood there with her hands on her hips, staring him down.

"Um," he started, completely unsure of what to say next, "Yes," he finished weakly.

She threw her arms in the air in exasperation, and then ordered him to sit down before he fell down. He did as he was told. "You'll get used to the smell soon enough, and then you won't even notice it. Are you hungry?" she said, but he noticed her tone had softened. She noticed her tone had softened too. She realized she had missed having companionship other than just the cow.

"Yes, I am," Forbes answered. "Is there something I can help with?"

His pro-offerance of help stopped Greer in her tracks, and she looked at him directly. "Do you know how to cook?" she asked. He wasn't sure if he heard doubt or hope in that question.

"A little," he answered with an embarrassed grin.

"I can handle tonight, and we can work out tomorrow's meals tomorrow," she replied and then set about making their dinner. Forbes really hoped she was going to clean her hands before handling their food, but he decided to be quiet about it.

He hadn't realized he had dozed off until he felt her shaking his feet. He awoke to the nice smell of food cooking, but he wasn't sure what kind of food. He realized that he had a blanket covering him as well. That surprised him. He sat up straighter, and then she asked him a question, "You sleep an awful lot, why?"

Forbes raised his eyebrows at her question. Then he rubbed his face in his hands and then his hands through his hair and then sat up even straighter and crossed his legs. "Yes, yes, I do," he answered. "And, well, I don't know exactly why. And whatever you're cooking smells nice. But as hungry as I am, I need to go relieve myself before we start eating." And with that said, he stood up and walked away from their camp to take care of things.

Greer had lived with a man her whole life, so she didn't understand why he had to announce it, but she set about serving up the meal. After they had finished their stew of sorts and had some mead that Greer had bartered for in the last town, they sat next to each other for a bit in a silence that was unexpectedly comfortable. They each had their own cartwheel to lean up against for support.

After the meal, Greer felt the same body needs as Forbes had earlier, so she simply got up and walked away from the cart. Forbes misread her movement.

"What? What did I do? Where are you going?" he asked with more concern in his voice than he had intended.

"I need to 'relieve myself'," she replied, using his same words so that they were clear on what she was going to do. Her reply caused him to blush and mumble to himself as she continued to walk away.

As she had a little time to herself away from him now, she thought about life. She had really only ever known one person her whole existence. It had been unnerving to hear about her life from an outside perspective. She wondered what her father, Carter, would have thought about all this. Maybe she had been reckless to go and confront this storyteller, but how could she not? She remembered what Carter had taught her and what she had heard in her story. Everything has a purpose. And if every "thing" had a purpose, then didn't it hold true that every "person" had a purpose too? Carter had known his purpose, but did she know hers?

If what she heard in her story was true, then she had come here for a purpose, but did she ever know what that purpose had been? Was it simply to be, or was there more to it? Well, she certainly wasn't going to find it standing out here in the dark and urinating. So she finished her "relieving" and then headed back to her camp and her new challenge of finding out who she was, and is, and why.

CHAPTER 4
Am I Crazy?

Forbes sat there against the cartwheel and wondered if he'd gone mad. What was he doing? He'd always known he was not as normal as the other storytellers, but being quirky was a helpful trait for a storyteller. His earliest memories of family and community and a world bigger than himself had always centered around storytelling. He had been captivated by the storyteller's voice, the cadence of the words and the pictures they formed in his mind's eye.

Every time the storyteller came to their area, the whole of the community of men would gather to hear a new story, a revised old story or a story told exactly the same overtime so that each member of the community could recite it from memory and yet still have a sense of surprise and delight. He knew from his youngest days that being a storyteller was his future because it was his passion.

He had gone to study with some of the great storytellers, but as great as his enthusiasm for the craft had been, he was not top of his class. His stories were fresh and innovative and popular, but also unconventional, untraditional and occasionally radical. Some of his peers called him dangerous as he told stories of love and females and togetherness. He was questioned often about how he knew of females, and what they felt and or thought. Was he breaking the law and/or in communication with them? Which is why he had been sent to the more remote communities to perform, which of course is how he came to be sitting here wondering if he was mad.

Why did he sleep so much? Actually, the better question was, why did he dream so much? Dare he share what he knew about himself with Greer even though it made no sense? But maybe she would be the one person who would believe him, since she'd know the truth of what he was telling her since he knew her story, and yet, how could he? His head was hurting with all these thoughts, so he put his head into his hands, which is when Greer walked back into camp.

She saw Forbes with his head in his hands, legs pulled in with his elbows resting on his knees, and she moved quickly to him, thinking he might be sick.

"Are you okay?" she asked, the concern clearly there in her question.

He pulled his hands away from his face to answer, and was unexpectedly face to face with her. This startled him so he jerked his head backwards too hard and slammed it into the cartwheel with a fair bit of force. "OW!" he exclaimed. "Well, I was until just now," he said, irritated, holding his head now from the back.

Greer plopped back from her squat to land on her bottom and sighed with exasperation. "Oh, what a pair we are," she said and then she started to laugh. It was kinda a little laugh, and then she couldn't stop laughing. She even tipped herself over onto her side and laughed so hard that tears came out and made clear little trails down her dirty face.

And then to his surprise, he started to laugh too. He didn't know why, but he laughed until he cried as well. Greer stopped laughing, though, when she noticed that there was blood on Forbes' hand that had been holding the back of his head. Greer quickly moved to get a clean rag and used the warm water for cleaning the dishes on the back of his head. He winced a little at her ministrations, but did no complaining.

She let him continue to hold the rag there on his head to maintain pressure while she finished cleaning up their meal. With that taken care of, she returned to his head. Luckily, the cut was small and would heal quickly. She rinsed out the blood and then threw the dirty water away from their camp.

Greer returned the items she used for the meal and his wound back into the cart and then returned with a fresh dung piece for the fire. She had been right, as soon as this new one caught fire, he didn't even notice the smell.

It seemed now that she might be up for conversation, so he started, "Do you know where we are?" It wasn't a great conversation starter, but he hoped it would lead to one anyway.

CHAPTER 5
The Conversation Begins

Greer realized that the best way over a river was a bridge, and that it seemed that honest conversation might create a bridge for them to build an understanding of this situation. She had so many questions, but she couldn't ask them all at once, so she started with the easiest answer to the easiest question, Where are they?

"Yes, I do know where we are, mostly," she started. "Clear as I can tell, this is the road that Carter took to find me. I have checked local community road charts and this one doesn't seem to be on any of them. And I don't know why exactly I 'feel' I need to go in this direction either. Before today, I thought I wanted to be around more people in communities, to learn what is there to learn since I'd never experienced that before. And, that I guess is why when I heard the tale of a storytelling event, I went to listen," she finished.

"Yes, well, meeting you was a shock to my system as well," he replied.

"Why did you fall asleep into your breakfast that way?" she asked, cutting straight to the point. He liked that about her.

"Well, okay," Forbes began, "Not sure if I can make sense of it to you since it makes no sense to me except that I know I do it so I'm used to it."

"Do you always make conversation so cryptic?" Greer asked.

Forbes looked at the expression on her face; it was somewhere between taunting and exasperation. So he sighed, and started again.

"Ok, be patient with me. Today one of my story characters walked up to me and said 'Hello.' This is not a usual occurrence. And then for our own safety we had to leave in some stealth. And then, we walked the whole day, not my usual amount of exercise, and then I banged my head up and laughed so hard I cried. It's been an unprecedented day!" And to his surprise, Greer smiled at him. A genuine and welcoming smile, and even though darkness was falling, he felt bathed in sunshine.

He realized he was staring at her, and he thought he felt a sideways grin on his face as he did. And she just sat there looking at him eagerly, almost childlike, waiting for him to speak. So he gathered his wits and began again, "Ok, so you wanted to know why I fell asleep into my breakfast." She nodded. "Well, sometimes, a feeling comes over me, and I can usually sense it, and put myself into a comfortable position before I fall asleep. But it is more than sleeping, it is a very real and vivid dream-sleep." He paused to see and hear her reaction.

Greer leaned back against her cartwheel, with a HMMM, and then turned to face him and asked, "So, what you're telling me is that nobody told you about me, my father or our life, you 'dreamt' it." Forbes shook his head in agreement. She continued, "So, when you fell asleep in your breakfast, and I sat watching you in the guest hut, you were dreaming?" Again Forbes nodded in agreement. She continued still, "So did you dream of me again?"

He sighed in relief, she was understanding him. "No, I didn't dream of you again. I dreamt of a girl named Meridal and a man named Robin Hood and of a magic golden arrow," Forbes said.

"Oh, I haven't heard that story before. Father didn't know that one. Will you tell me?" Greer asked eagerly. Forbes smiled to himself, because it was the perfect way to illustrate to her what she herself had witnessed and so he agreed.

At the end of the story, Forbes opened up his small, worn black leather backpack and emptied out the contents. In and amongst the many odd items, there was a beautiful and tiny golden arrow with its four golden roses that gleamed in the firelight. She didn't ask for permission, she just reached for it, having to prove it was real. With the arrow in her hand, she asked another question, "How?" But she already knew his answer, so he simply just shrugged his shoulders with his hands up, in the universal sign of 'I don't know.'

Greer returned the treasure to his pile. Then she looked at him, all the childlike wonder replaced with steely determination and said, "There is something at work here bigger than you or I." Forbes simply shook his head in agreement. The day's activities, both physical and mental, were catching up fast on him. Greer noticed he was too tired for more talk so she encouraged him to get comfortable and sleep. She didn't know if sleeping and dreaming were restful to him in equal shares or not, but she hoped he would be rested in the morning because she had more questions and there was more distance to cover.

Greer herself was not ready for sleep just yet, so many thoughts bustling around in her head. So she focused on making sure the little camp was secure and that Jow was happy before she herself crawled into her sleeping spot.

As she lay there with her eyes open, looking at the last dying embers of the dung fire, she thought of her father. Her father had told her of the uniqueness of their beginning, and yet she never thought of herself as unique. She simply was. She didn't have much experience with other people, but she didn't feel like Forbes was untrustworthy. Hadn't he risked his own life by leaving with her? As she watched the last embers of the fire, she asked herself if she believed in magic. Mustn't she? If not, how could any of this make sense? She herself saw her father in the flames. She herself heard Forbes tell a story he couldn't possibly know. She herself had heard a voice other than her own in her head. But she needed rest, so she herself told herself to go to sleep. And Greer listened.

Sometime before dawn, when everything was still damp with the night fog, Greer awoke to a sound she didn't recognize. She lay there alert and motionless for a moment or two to get a sense of if there was danger. She breathed a sigh of relief. It was only the stirrings of her new traveling companion. She looked over to see Forbes twitching and moving like he was somewhere doing something. She realized he was dreaming again. She was not ready to be out of her own blankets, so she tucked herself back under them now that she knew they were in no danger. She heard Forbes say a word, "Christmas," out loud. 'Christmas' she thought, not recognizing the word or having any context for its meaning. Well, she had really enjoyed listening to Forbes tell her story as well as Meridal's, so she guessed rightly he was dreaming a story, and looked forward to having something to listen to at their next meal. And she wondered excitedly what would show up in his bag. Then she surrendered herself back to sleep.

The Christmas Wish

———— ··•·· ————

This time of year, everyone's self-interest becomes alert. "What do you want for Christmas?" is the question on everyone's mind and lips. No doubt you rattle off about some 'thing' you want over and above any of the real and necessary things one needs for life. Or, maybe that list of things is a necessity for you?

Anyway this year is different - no reason, only different. There is a young woman from a very comfortable family. She is attractive and well-liked by peers. Usually, her biggest worry is what to wear, and if she will or won't be invited to this or that party. She wants 'wants' for Christmas, tons of them and of course, she knows she'll get them too. Her life seems to be all she ever wanted, but still she wants more.

With only nine days of Christmas shopping left, she decides it is time to go and do her own shopping for others. At the mall, there are the usual rude mobs of holiday shoppers. She thinks to herself, "People are so rude this time of year. Holiday shopping brings out all the worst in people - I'm glad it's only once a year. But,....I do love the presents!"

That's what Christmas means to her—presents. This year she will be getting one she needs and doesn't even know she wants.

On the way home, she stops at an expensive, and trendy, croissant and expresso shop to relax. While she sits there at a table by the window, she watches all the people go by, wondering why they rush to and fro.

"They rush around hoping to find what they want before someone else snatches it away from them," a creaky old voice answers her unvoiced question from behind her. Startled, she gives a little jump in her chair and then turns around to look at who has spoken to her. She looks right into the face of the ugliest old woman, almost hag-like, that she has ever seen.

Trying to be charming, but coming off sarcastic, she replies, "Why, thank you for that unique insight." Then, she abruptly turns back around to face her own table, looking out the window once more, hoping she has dissuaded further conversation.

But the old woman continues in her smug, raspy voice, "It's not unique, this insight of mine."

The young woman, now not wanting to lose her patience, turns back around to the old woman and says, "Thank you, again. Please, I am trying to be alone and relax." And then, hoping she has had the final word, abruptly turns back to her table and window-watching once more.

"You don't have to try to be alone...," the smug, raspy old woman's voice trails off, almost taunting her.

This time the young woman will not be polite. Turning back around, she starts, "Really, if you don't mind...," but she never finishes her sentence. The old woman's table is empty. She looks around the small cafe. No one even seems aware that she is sitting there. Terribly uncomfortable now, she drinks her last sip of expresso and leaves, croissant unfinished on her table.

The rest of the day, she wonders about the strange encounter at the cafe.

At home that evening, the old hag's words seem to haunt her thoughts, "You don't have to try to be alone." She rummages through her house, trying to find something else to occupy her thoughts.

She finally gives up and makes herself a cup of soothing tea and goes up to her bedroom.

In her room, she sits on her bed looking around the room without really looking at anything. Her eyes finally fix upon an item of interest though. She gets up and walks to her bureau. Hidden behind bottles of unused, expensive parfums is her diary. Now, this is something she hasn't thought about in years. Opening it to the last entry, December 16th, 1989. Five years? It has been a long time. She takes the diary back to her bed and decides to read what she had thought, and done in her life.

She had started the journal when she was just twenty-one, right out of college. Now at age twenty-eight, she realizes how little she has either written or done. Reading through it makes her laugh, and cry, and think about herself. When she finishes reading, it is well into the early morning. She sighs, turns off the light and falls asleep. But before falling asleep, she decides she will return to the cafe to see if the old woman (hag, she thought to herself) would be there again. She doesn't know why, she just knows she wants to see.

The next day comes, and at about the same time as the day before, she ventures back into the cafe. She sits down at the same table by the window. She has her usual order in front of her. She looks around the cafe, instead of out of the window. The cafe is crowded today, but there is no old hag lurking anywhere to be seen. Well, she thinks to herself, a chance encounter and she isn't going to let it bother her anymore. It was just some lonely old woman looking to make someone else feel as bad as she does.

"That's usually how it works," says a gentle, elderly voice from behind her. The young woman turns quickly around towards the voice, and now finds herself face to face with the most beautiful older woman she has ever seen. Grace simply flows from her. She is simply, but elegantly dressed, and smiling at her.

The young woman isn't prepared for this, so she simply says, "Pardon?"

The beautiful woman continues, "Yes, unhappy people usually don't want happy people around them. It makes them aware of their unhappiness and inadequacies."

The young woman is sure she had not been speaking out loud but rather only to herself in her mind. Her next question reflects her continued confusion, "Why do you say this to me?"

The graceful woman smiles, and a little tinkling sound of laughter comes gently from her as she says, "Well, because honey, you want to know." The young woman tries to interrupt after hearing this statement, but the older woman puts up her hand gently to quiet her and then continues speaking, "What do you want for Christmas?"

The young woman hears this question, and immediately her mind starts generating a list of all the material wants/things in her head.

The graceful woman continues, and gently admonishes her as if she were a small child, "No, no, no dear." And then the older woman reaches out a warm hand to the young woman's hand as if to calm her. "What do you want for Christmas? What does it mean to you?"

Again, the questions generate images and thoughts of rushing and rude shoppers, parties, opening presents, all the glitter, TV specials, and then somewhere in the back of her mind, she remembers family, friends, Santa Claus, church and Jesus Christ's birth. She remembers giving, the real spirit of Christmas. As her thoughts flow into these deeper thoughts, she feels the older woman's comforting hand give hers a little squeeze and then some pats that she is getting it right.

"Yes," the older woman continues. "That is what Christmas means. There are two types of ways to be in the world. You have seen them both. Which do you want?"

The young woman closes her eyes, takes in a breath, and thinks to herself. Of course she wants to be beautiful and graceful and gentle and loved. She comes out of her thoughts and opens her eyes, fully expecting to see the beautiful woman she has been talking to, well, sort of talking to, but there in front of her sits the hag! And her smile is anything but beautiful.

"That's what I always wanted too, but never what I needed. He, He he! Always what I wanted...." the hag almost cackles in her laughter.

The young woman quickly pulls her hand back and spins away from the old hag, frightened beyond fright. She must be asleep, she tells herself. She gets up quickly from the table, deciding to walk straight out of this daymare. She doesn't even look behind her as she exits the cafe. She knows if she does, the table behind hers would have been empty.

Thoughts, flowing and ebbing, of her life fill her dreams that night. When she awakens in the morning, she finds those same thoughts still with her, leaving her senses dull. She has a very slow and thoughtful cup of coffee that morning.

Eventually her senses wake up, and the thoughts stop their complete domination of her consciousness. Looking in the mirror before her shower, though, she feels as if she is looking at someone else. Who is this person that she has created for the world to behold? Is it really her at all? She shrugs off her bathrobe, wishing she could do as much with her thoughts. She steps in the shower to hide.

"You don't have to try to be alone," the old hag's words haunt her still. She could hear them echoing throughout and over all thoughts. A feeling of extreme loneliness overcomes her, then a revelation.

She has created a shell to hide in and keep herself safe. What she has really created doesn't protect or shield her from the world, but the other way round, it shields the world from her. She could die and no one would note her passing—she has made no mark on others' lives, consequentially, allowing them no way to mark hers. Reading through her own diary two nights before, she has remembered how carefree and open she had been —how in love with life we are in our younger selves.

"YOU DON'T HAVE TO TRY TO BE ALONE." Now she understands what Christmas means, what life means. She wants to share experiences, and laughter and joy. She wants to love people more than wanting them to love her. This time of year, it depends upon whose eyes you are looking through, she supposes.

"What do I want for Christmas?" She smiles to herself. She hugs her naked, wet body under the running water. And she laughs. And she cries.

"What do I want for Christmas?" She wants everyone to realize what she'd realize. Life without living, laughing and loving is death, and death is meaningless if there are no warm memories of your life kept in people's hearts. That is the truest gift.

And somewhere in the world, both a beautiful and ugly old woman smile at each other, and sit together and share coffee and warm memories of their lives. For eternity...

CHAPTER 6

Getting to Know One Another

When morning came, Forbes found that Greer was already up and about, and that a new dung fire was cheerfully warming him. He smiled to himself. He sat up, drew his legs into his body and hugged his knees. He knew he had dreamt a new story, and this story made him feel happy and hopeful inside. Usually, he knew what he'd find in his backpack, but this time he didn't, and he found that excited him. He would look later. Right now, he just sat in his contentment.

Greer had noticed that Forbes had awakened, but wasn't really moving. Maybe his head injury was worse than she had thought. She went over to where she had had her sleeping space and sat down.

He looked over at her and gave her a sleepy smile. She wasn't sure what that meant. Her father had never given her sleepy smiles like that. So instead of trying to guess what he might be thinking, she asked him, "Are you okay?"

To which he simply nodded his head in affirmation, with that sleepy smile still on his face. So Greer thought she'd try a different tactic. "What's Christmas?" That seemed to get this attention. He seemed awake now. And he seemed to have found his voice once again.

"How do you know about Christmas?" he asked.

"I don't know about Christmas. That's why I am asking you," she replied. He had to smile to himself again. She was infuriating to have a conversation with and yet, he couldn't help himself since all he wanted to do was talk to her.

"Why are you smiling?" she asked. "Are you feeling okay? You hit your head pretty hard last night. Maybe we should find a community village that has a healer?" she asked selfishly, not wanting to have another dead man in her camp.

"Yes, yes, Greer. I am fine. I had a dream last night that left me feeling elated. And it was about Christmas, and I can't figure out how you know that," he said finally.

"Oh, well, I can tell you how I know the word Christmas. You said it out loud last night before dawn. You were thrashing about in your sleep, and since that was a new sound, it woke me up. I heard you say the word out loud before I fell back asleep. I'd never heard the word before so I wondered what you were talking about. I could tell by your twitching that you were dreaming, and not just sleeping," she said plainly. Then she continued, "Why don't you go and 'relieve yourself' and then after you return, you can tell me the story you dreamt while I get our breakfast ready and take care of Jow?"

Forbes could tell by the hopefulness in her voice that she was eager to hear another story. It sounded like a fair trade to him. He really wasn't much of a cook. He agreed.

Later that day, they had moved on from their last campsite. Greer seemed deep in thought about his last story. He wasn't sure what had her so deep in thought. He had never really considered that people might think about his stories once he told them. He was more accustomed to being concerned about the cheering at the end; he paid no more thought to what happened after. What an interesting concept, that maybe, maybe his stories had meaning to others beyond pure pleasure and entertainment. Now, he found himself in deep thought as well, as they wandered, it seemed, towards a destination neither of them had any idea about.

Their day progressed rather the same as their past days, so he figured this was the new normal. Walk in thought and silence, stop when she decided they had arrived, and then set up camp and talk, eat, sleep and start all over again. Why was he traveling with her again? He still wasn't sure, but still, here he was with her.

Greer had decided upon a stopping place that looked more or less the same as the others. She set about doing what she was accustomed to, and he went to find a stone big enough to sit upon, which he found rather easily.

Greer watched him walk off a bit to have a seat. She sighed, he still wasn't much help around camp, but it was his company and storytelling that she craved. She let him alone.

Forbes sat on the rock and looked over at her. She was a puzzle to him. What did he really know about a woman though? What did he really know about anybody? Only what he had "dreamt" of. He sat there lost in his thoughts, and as he watched her, to his eyes, or anyone's eyes, she looked like a man. She acted like a man. She definitely smelled worse than most men he'd ever come into contact with. And he considered that maybe his fascination with her lay in the fact that he alone knew she wasn't a man.

He wondered still how and why she had confronted him, and why he continued to follow her. And where were they headed??

He suddenly felt as if he was being watched, and this brought him back to the present. He looked up and realized Greer was no longer moving in her natural methodical way while she put camp together, but rather looking very intently at him. He was about to complain that he had a right to sit and be with his thoughts after a long day of walking when she held up a hand in caution to be silent.

All of his senses were alert now. His eyes watched her.

Greer stood near her cart, but not near enough to touch it. She had lowered her body to a semi-crouch in anticipation of the attack she knew would come. She knew there was more than one of them out there. And she guessed they had been followed since the last hamlet community where she had traded for supplies and met the storyteller.

Greer wasn't sure if Forbes had any fight training like that which she had received from her father, but she hoped he could handle himself. She noticed that he had been slowly moving himself forward on the boulder upon which he had been idly sitting just a moment before. Good, she thought to herself. He knows we are not alone. She could see him settling his feet more firmly on the ground and readying himself to move quickly. This gave her confidence that he understood that threat was coming.

The creeping men must have realized that they had lost their element of surprise and cried out a battle call as they charged. Four burley men armed with quarterstaffs burst out from the shrubbery that had been their cover and came in for the attack.

Forbes watched as it all seemed to happen in slow motion, as a man much larger than Greer ran full speed toward her with his staff raised. Greer stood her ground, ready. And as the man moved to swing his staff at her, she went low and tackled him as he left his middle exposed. As she held on to him, she ran full steam into her cart with a solid thud, knocking the wind out of him and causing him to drop his staff, which she fluidly picked up. Then, she smacked him in his head, before he regained his breath, and down he went. Out cold.

Forbes had heard the battle cry from behind him and ducked low using the boulder for cover and came up on the other side. His attacker, momentarily confused, gave Forbes all the time he needed to throw gritty dirt in the attacker's eyes and then follow up with a strong kick to his middle, causing his staff to fall as well. Forbes wasted no time in picking it up and giving a downward THWAK upon the doubled-over man in front of him.

Armed with a staff now as well as Greer, the two of them moved closer together and stood to face the next two attackers. The last two attackers seemed less eager to fight now that two of their comrades were already down.

Greer sensing their wariness, called out to them in a gruff voice laced with steel that Forbes didn't recognize, and said, "Well, do we dance? Or do you want to take your friends and go?"

Her brashness and readiness for battle unnerved the last two standing attackers. The would-be attackers cautiously laid down their staffs, and moved to each retrieve one of the fallen. Then they quickly retreated, leaving behind their weapons and moved back the way they had come.

Forbes looked in bewilderment at Greer, now that the danger had passed. She looked at him, still steely voiced and said, "Pack up, we're leaving now."

Forbes nodded, and moved to gather up the other two staffs and return loose items to the cart. After he had tucked everything in tightly, Greer re-hitched the cow. They were on the move in minutes.

This time it seemed Greer picked a very deliberate path on the hard ground to leave as little a trail as possible to follow in case those brutes thought about settling the score. She walked with Forbes following until well after nightfall. And as they made camp that night, there was no comfort of a dung fire, or a meal, except for the cow.

That night there was no sleep.

As the two of them sat alert and aware of their surroundings, Forbes noticed for the first time that the night was not silent. There was a difference in the sounds he heard now than during the day. How could he have lived so many years and missed so much of the world?

He was realizing that this journey with Greer was an education, allowing him to experience newness for himself rather than solely as an observer and storyteller.

He remembered a dream/story he hadn't shared yet with anyone because he didn't understand the context. Now in his newly-found self-chosen freedom from normal situations, he began to understand. He let his mind drift into his memory, knowing that Greer would keep vigilant. The dream-memory unfolded before him again.

Easy Way OUT

———— · ·●· · ————

The wind blows wildly outside. I sit inside, safe from the brewing storm. Safe? Hah! I shudder within my robe. What a day. Trapped here when all I want is to do is run away. Escape. Where would I even go if I could? Nowhere. I had been looking for a shortcut and, unlucky for me, I found it. I had been too blind to see what my life would be like if I gave it away.

I have never tried to be anything in my life. I have always looked for the easy way out. Well, whoever named it "easy" didn't know much, not at all. So here I am, locked into a fate I brought upon myself because of my unwillingness to go into the world and try to be somebody, even if that only meant being myself. Instead, now, I just exist in a sort of nowhere zone. Today, though, it seems for the first time, even though it's a little late in coming, I am unhappy enough to do something about it. The big question: WHAT?

If I leave him and this life, where do I go? I don't have any job skills that I can think of, or even a complete high school education. The only thing I can think of to be thankful for is that I have no children. He, this Prince Charming of mine, would beat me to a pulp if he knew I have been purposely avoiding getting pregnant. And, another "thank you God," because we have never been officially married.

I realize I have some advantages on my side. This gives me hope. I still have my fantasies about meeting a guy who is on the up and up. Drugs. I can't believe that I didn't know that was his business.

Actually, I can. I didn't want to know. All I wanted to know was that he was rich enough to give me all the things I thought were important. And, I lied to myself that the bruises were my fault. Well, I'm not lying to myself anymore.

The wind howls outside, causing me to shudder again. Escape. Yeah, that would be nice, wouldn't it?

The clock in the living room chimes 6:30 AM. I'd better start the coffee and breakfast. I didn't need another of his bad moods. I guess the illegal drug business lately isn't as good as normal. With all the international conflicts going on, he's been having trouble with his shipments. The cops are starting to take more notice of him too. As I turn on the coffee pot, I wonder how I had been able to turn such a blind eye to the truth of him. Now, it all seems so obvious. Hindsight? Enough rumination, time to make breakfast. Let's see, maybe some French Toast? Yeah, that'd be great on such a stormy morning.

I hear his alarm buzz in the bedroom. He'll take his shower and then he'll want breakfast. That gives me about thirty-five minutes to have it ready.

He eats quickly and quietly, absorbed in some newspaper article. He gives me his customary list of daily chores to have done before he returns home from work. He leaves without his usual goodbye, very unusual.

I clear up his breakfast dishes, then sit down to eat my breakfast. I search through the newspaper eager to find the article he had been so interested in. Aha, here it is. Oh, now this is interesting.

"Drug Runners Running Scared in the County," heads the article. Well, my guess had been on target. The cops are getting close. What would happen to me, I wonder? Would I be held as an accomplice? With my luck, probably. Then the thought really sinks in, and I sit back into the chair with a worried frown on my face. I will. What would I do then? There would be no escape.

I look at the list of chores on the table and then push it away in an act of defiance. I know now that I have no more time to lament my choices and I have to act now to save myself or forever hold my peace of this awful life.

I want something better. "I will not be caged," I declare out loud as an image of a bird being freed from its birdcage fills my mind and heart with hope.

I rush into the bedroom and find my suitcase. I wipe my hand across my face. Tears? For what? Self-pity or fear? Did it matter?

In a frantic flurry, I stuff my suitcase with all the things I can fit. I take a brief shower and quickly dress. Oh God! What if he comes home for some reason? Be brave, I tell myself. It's about time that you stood on your own two feet. Where are mothers when you really need them? Where was mine ever? I guess she is right where I pushed her, away from me. Hard luck story, huh? I could hear the violins in the background.

Reaching under the floorboards in the bedroom closet, I carefully pull out an old shoebox containing my only savings. I have almost $1500. Well, this will get me somewhere. The plane fares seem to be really low right now.

I call a taxi. It takes only about 15 minutes to get here. I scribble a quick note on the newspaper, near the article, saying goodbye. It is still early, so I hope that none of the nosy neighbors will notice me slipping away. A slight smile crosses my lips. Could I almost taste freedom? It is pretty wonderful, but I am not free. Not yet. I still have to get somewhere he'll never think of. Good thing he was never that interested in knowing who I am, maybe it's a good thing I never really got to know who I am either.

As the taxi driver takes me to the airport, I drift back into my childhood memories. What had I wanted to be when I grew up? My mind fills with childhood dreams and wishes. Dreams of being famous. Dreams of being rich. Dreams of being a beauty to make men swoon. Dreams of being bright and intelligent and sought after not only for beauty, but for wit and character as well. Dreams of glamour and romance. I realize those are not my dreams anymore. This moment, as I reach for freedom, I dream of respect for myself and from others. I wish to be taken for the person I am inside...or at least for the person I want to become. We are at the airport before I know it.

I pay the cabby and thank him for the ride. He had talked the whole way, and I hadn't heard a word of it. Oh well, I guess he is used to it. As the cab drives away, leaving me alone, I stand and look around for where I want to go. Freedom. Anywhere that isn't too expensive or crowded. I decide. Looking at a map, I see something I like. There! Yeah, that will do nicely. The ticket counter had no line. The flight is not expensive and just far enough to be away. I am going to disappear...and then find myself.

I purchase the ticket and give the airline agent my luggage. I buy coach, needing to save every penny. The flight will be moderately long and I hope pleasant. I sit next to a younger girl on her way to college. As we talk, I could see in her face all the dreams of the future, hers and mine. So much energy, so much faith, hope and honesty. Is that what I had given up looking for the easy way out? I swallow hard. If only...Well, I have taken the first step forward. I am learning to walk, and soon I will be running. She knows so much about the world and people. I am fascinated by her insight. As the flight comes to an end, she smiles at me and thanks me for a wonderful flight. Me! I have no words to express my gratitude to her, so I simply return her warm smile. I have looked into a mirror and seen what I can be. What I will be!

After disembarking the plane, I watch everyone being greeted by friends or loved ones. Funny, I don't feel lonely. I have some of my self-respect back. So I have gotten a little sidetracked in life, now I have found the strength to walk straight.

I walk determinedly through the airport, take a taxi to the nearest motel and get a newspaper. After checking in, I go straight to my room and search through the Want Ads. What had I wanted to be when I grew up? I smile broadly now. I had wanted to be ME! Now, NOW, I have a chance to find out who that can be.

··●··

Jow's bell rings softly, Forbes smiles as he stirs from his thoughts, feeling a kinship with the woman choosing to find out who she truly is.

CHAPTER 7

Asking More Questions

Forbes usually had no trouble sleeping through the night. But after the recent ambush, the constant moving of their camp, and his fascination with Greer, he did wonder what he was doing. He had just recently achieved a higher status in the storytelling guild, and had been getting used to all of the celebrity his stories were bringing to him, and now he is sleeping in the dirt under an old blanket and smelling of dung fire smoke. Why had he chosen to follow her? But he knew the answer before he had even asked himself the question...what storyteller doesn't love a mystery? And, he was beginning to realize that cages come in all sorts of disguises.

He knew he was on the fringe with his inventive and fanciful stories of places no one had even conceived of before. He also knew he challenged authority by telling these stories. They were allowed simply because the authorities deemed his stories so fanciful that no one would find truth in them. And, you know, he thought to himself, maybe I would think they were all part of my imagination too, if it wasn't for all those little story-trinket souvenirs that showed up after a "story" dream. And then, now, A PERSON! A real life, breathing person, who he only thought was a character. How could he not follow her?

But following her wasn't getting him any closer to answers, only more and more questions. So here he was in the middle of the night, under a sky full of stars, and he was wide awake.

Greer's story, and the story of her father, the Carter, were all about finding purpose. At least the way he dreamt it and told it. That was the takeaway message for him. So what was his purpose? To tell stories? To entertain? To gain fame? Or was there something bigger here as Greer had suggested? If her purpose as a carter was to find uses for things, then he should like to think of what his purpose is all about.

One thing made very clear by being with Greer out in the wild was that he was technically unskilled. He has had others do things for him his whole life. Like cooking. And sewing. And most recently, fighting. Greer can teach him these things. He realized he wants to be more able to care for himself in more situations. He discovered he envied that about her. She has such determination as well as curiosity.

She is always asking questions. And when she isn't, she's watching him and seemingly gaining understanding that way. Well, he watches her too. But he's not sure if it's just for gaining understanding...or, maybe in a way, it is.

He sees what she wants the world to see when they look at her. She walks like a man, has male mannerisms, is in constant need of a bath, but he also sees what she doesn't realize is not there. She has no beard, and although nearly the same height as himself, she is still too slight to be taken as full-grown and therefore will always be treated as a young adult. If they stay together, a brother scenario, older and younger, may serve them well. And that thought there stopped all the others.

He laid there looking up at the stars, and felt his heart pounding so loud it was in his ears. He realized he had been holding his breath. So he let his breath out slowly and breathed in an even and steady one. He wanted to protect her.

He wanted to protect her, and that thought surprised him. And almost at the same moment that he realized this thought, a brilliant shooting star moved across the sky. Awe and wonder.

Why did he want to protect her? It was just made very plainly to him that she could take care of herself after she trounced those road thugs. She was the one protecting and caring for him. He decided he had thought about enough things tonight, so he readjusted his body, and he did fall asleep. He didn't dream.

··●··

Greer almost always woke before dawn, and today was no exception. Forbes almost always slept until after sun up. At first this schedule had irritated her, almost as if he purposely was trying to get out of morning camp activities, but now she welcomed the time to herself. It also gave her a chance to investigate the contents of his daypack. She was a scavenger of sorts, so she didn't exactly see it as an invasion of his property or privacy. She always put everything back in.

There were several items she didn't have any association for, so she left those alone. The items she was interested in were the ones that had shown up after the stories he had told her since she met him. Her favorite item to date was the tiny golden arrow with four roses on it. It had no real purpose as a weapon, and its only obvious purpose was as an adornment, but she wondered why someone would want to adorn themselves with something of no real use. The second item that had shown up was the Christmas gift box. She loved the colors of it, sky blue and white like clouds, and when she opened it up to look inside, even though she knew there'd never be anything inside, she always had swirls in her stomach in anticipation. And the latest item was a small silver bell with the design of a cage etched onto it. The tinkling sound it made delighted her and it was a sound similar to her cow's bell, only so much more delicate. She only rang it once because she didn't want to wake Forbes and have him discover her rummaging in his bag.

She looked at these items, and included herself, and wondered what it all meant. What was the purpose of this all? Was it simply so she would have a traveling companion once more? She did like having his company. He was interesting, although not extremely helpful. But she could tell that he was trying to learn new skills, and that made her smile. She imagined her father would be welcoming of her teaching the skills he taught her to someone else.

She carefully replaced the items into his bag. The sun would be rising soon, and he would wake up. After putting each item back into his bag and closing it up and returning it to the spot he had left it last night, she rolled up her blanket. She walked off a little distance to relieve herself before returning to camp to make the fire and get breakfast for the cow, herself and Forbes.

Forbes, who had been silently watching her, watched her walk off and couldn't contain the smile on his face. Her curiosity delighted him. He thought what fun it would be if he hid items in the gift box for her to find? But decided against it for the moment. He enjoyed knowing something about her that she didn't think anyone knew.

When Greer returned she was surprised. Sitting with a grin so big was Forbes in front of a nicely burning dung fire, with water almost to a boil. Greer couldn't help but smile back at him.

"Well, it seems this day is off to a brilliant start," she said as she moved to the back of the cart to sort the oats for cooking.

"Any dreams?" she asked him.

"Nope, not last night," he answered.

"Hmm," she sighed. He thought he sensed disappointment. So he asked, "What is today all about? More traveling or foraging or…" but he was interrupted from any more ideas by Greer.

"Today is about combat training," she announced with a smile as she returned to mix the oats into the now-boiling water. She continued to smile as she stirred.

"Oh," replied Forbes, a bit less enthusiastically than when he had voiced his other suggestions, "that sounds painful."

"Oh, don't fret, I don't want to thump you. I want to make sure you're the one doing the thumping should the need ever arise again."

"Hey, I didn't do so badly last time," he retorted.

"No, you didn't," she agreed. "But, in the event it happens again, we need to have a better idea of our fighting strengths."

Forbes couldn't argue with that...but after the long day of training he might have wished he had.

Later that night, as they sat somewhat together after their meal by the dung fire, Forbes watched with great interest as Greer, seemingly distracted by thoughts she voiced out loud all the while, used her belt knife to cut off pieces of her hair and put those pieces into the fire where they made little instant sizzling blazes. She was curious about so many things and always, since he'd known her, wanted to know more and understand why.

"So you have never seen an alive female? I mean before me?" she asked.

Forbes had a short stick he'd been whittling at with his own belt knife, and was using the now pointy, slim stick to draw patterns in the soft dirt in front of him. At her question, he sort of paused in his pattern making, pursed his lips together and seemed to look off into the memories in his mind's eye of his past years. Greer was used to this reaction from Forbes now when she asked a question of him, so she gave him the time he needed before she would get an answer. While she waited, she kept working on her hair cutting. She didn't have to wait too long.

"When I was really young," he started, "I remember a stone building, all cold and damp. I think I was there to get tested, or something like that, because after that memory, I went to live at the Storyteller's Guild School. But as I stood in a hallway, I remember hearing a swishing sound a ways down the hall, so I turned to look and I briefly saw a figure in a long gown move across the corridor into an adjacent hallway. I'd never seen anyone wear a gown like that before or since. I guess that was a woman, maybe." He finished his memory recall with a shrug of his shoulders and then resumed his pattern making in the soft dirt. But Greer, of course, had more questions.

"So, the only females/women you've ever 'seen' have been in your dreams? But then, where do those ideas come from on what a female looks like? If you have no reference point besides a swishing gown?" she asked, but Forbes could hear the frustration behind her question. So, he asked one of his own questions in response.

"Greer, what you really want to know is who you are. I don't know that answer. I don't know how I even know about your story. I don't know why I dream fantastical stories about fantastical places and people - male and female. And," he paused here for effect because he's a storyteller after all, "why objects arrive in my daypack mysteriously as story-trinket souvenirs!" And with that said, Forbes stood up and walked out of the fire's circle of light.

Surprised by him, Greer called out, "Where are you going?" she asked.

His response made her giggle, "To relieve myself."

She used this time alone to finish up on her hair. She put her knife down on a nearby stone she had been using as a table of sorts and then used her fingers to check the length of her hair that she had been accustomed to wearing. She smiled to herself because she seemed to be getting the hang of this hair-cutting thing. Then, she sighed a big sigh. She missed Carter, her father. She smiled again at the memory of her first haircut she gave to him, after extensive practice on the cow's tail. She'd cut his ear a bit, and as she fretted about hurting him, he turned it around and into a learning opportunity for wound care. She was distracted by her memories as she heard footsteps coming towards her. Unworried, she gave her hair and head one more shake and then stood up to brush stray hairs from her clothing. She began to reach for her belt knife down on the low rock, then paused, all senses alert.

She had heard footsteps.

Forbes had been gone far too long to relieve himself.

There was danger.

She knew she could not go for her knife, but there was the fire, and the heavy cooking pan. And as Greer stood there in that moment of indecision before action, she heard a thud, and then the sound of a body falling to the ground.

She swung herself into action, low and around the fire pit and came up with the cooking pan in hand and in a fighting stance to face the danger. But the face she saw across the fire was Forbes, holding a flat stone in one hand and stanching the blood on the side of his head with the other hand.

She dropped the pan and moved swiftly over to him, and helped him back in the firelight and leant up against his wagon wheel.

"What happened?" she asked in low tones.

"Make sure that person won't hurt us first," he ordered.

In agreement, Greer regained her belt knife, and then moved to the back of the cart, emptied out a burlap sack of its contents and grabbed a rope. She moved to put the sack over the head, shoulders and arms of their would-be-attacker, but not before she recognized his face. It was the youth who had been assigned to attend to Forbes at the storytelling event where she had met him.

She secured the sack with the extra rope she had made from worn-out sacks and tied it around his body and then his legs. This person wasn't going anywhere once they awoke.

Then she moved back to attend to Forbes' newest head wound, which he seemed to get with some disturbing frequency, she thought. After he was bandaged and she was fairly sure he wasn't seriously hurt, she told him who was in the sack.

"It's the boy attendant from the storytelling event where I met you," Greer said.

"Whaaat?" responded Forbes, finding it a bit harder than usual to think at the moment.

"Maybe he got into more trouble than you thought he would, and he came looking for you to save himself?" Greer offered up a possible scenario.

Forbes sighed. "Why is everything so complicated lately?" was all he said before he lost consciousness.

Greer sat back on her heels in front of him and responded, "Ain't that the truth."

Forbes had no choice but to go where his sleeping dream would take him.

The Guardian and the Gate

———— ··●·· ————

Erenow sits in her favorite chair, or at least what she remembers as her favorite chair, but she finds no comfort. She tries moving her body, or what she remembers of her body, to find a more comfortable position. Still unable to find comfort, she stands and begins to pace about the space she has remembered as her room. Where is she? Why can't she seem to remember? And when she tries to remember, then comes the pain. But why?

Another figure enters her "room" and seeks to comfort her.

"Erenow, why are you troubled?" a voice both distant and present asks. Erenow turns to face her questioning guest and finds Aeolian there. She begins to relax, as she always does when in the presence of Aeolian. Erenow knows she is safe, so she answers honestly.

"Why am I here? Who am I? Why do I remember some things like my favorite chair and room (even though they are unreal and without substance)? Why do I have no substance? And why does it hurt when I try to remember or think about these questions?" Erenow finishes.

Aeolian smiles at her young friend. Aeolian is the reason she is here, so she feels responsible for Erenow. She had misjudged how difficult the transition would be for Erenow. This bothers her, and she thinks that maybe the time has come to risk telling the whole truth.

Aeolian leads Erenow back to her favorite chair and then seats herself in a nearby chair. She speaks softly, "Erenow, there is a telling that I can tell, but it is not without risk to you. Do I have permission to tell?"

Erenow is confused by this question. Her hand instinctively and protectively goes to her midsection as a steadying gesture. Then, with her eyes firmly on the eyes of Aeolian, answers, "Yes."

Aeolian reassures her with a smile, then begins the telling.

As she begins, the rooms where they sit shifts from pale and veiled colors to bright and vivid ones and the sounds are no longer muffled, and the smells and physical sensations all seem to be assaulting Erenow all at once. She puts her hands over her ears and closes her eyes tightly shut and crunches her body over as she cries out.

And then, everything is stillness once more.

Erenow tentatively removes her hands from covering her ears, and opens her eyes, and straightens her body back up into the chair in a normal sitting posture. The world as she has come to know it has returned to normal. Sitting there across from her is Aeolian, very calm and smiling kindly.

Then Aeolian asks, "Do you want me to continue?"

Erenow answers, "Is this the risk you spoke of?"

Aeolian considers this question carefully before answering, "This is one of them."

"One of them?" Erenow responds with alarm. "There's more?"

"Yes," answers Aeolian.

"Why does there have to be pain?" Erenow cries.

Aeolian answers calmly, "Because Truth doesn't consider whether or not it makes you feel good or bad, it simply is what it is. The emotion we attach to Truth is what brings us pain or pleasure or ambivalence or peace."

Erenow looks at her friend Aeolian and says out loud, "Most of the time I don't understand what you're talking about."

Aeolian smiles again and responds, "I know." Then she continues, "But you will never have peace until you face your Truth. Without facing it, you will never move forward. Part of your Truth is that you are here because of me. I could not bear your suffering, and I offered you an escape from that pain. I had forgotten that no matter the distance, you cannot outrun pain. The only way is to face it, move through it, and find ways to love and forgive."

Erenow understands these words. "You're the reason I am so unhappy?" she fires the accusation at Aeolian.

Aeolian remains calm and unshaken as she answers, "No, I am not. But I did delay your sense of unhappiness. You will not find what you need to heal under this veil I have placed you in. Prepare yourself," Aeolian says with a force in her voice that Erenow has not heard before. And as Aeolian finishes speaking, before Erenow could respond, the veil is ripped away and Erenow begins watching herself from faraway and up close.

Part 1 - In the Castle Keep

The weather seems locked in gloom. Will Spring ever come? Sigh. I've sat mostly in my chamber on the top floor of this castle keep day after day, looking out of the window, hoping to see some evidence of Spring's onset. This morning, when I awoke though, the sunshine was glorious. But it has turned to a drizzly, stormy mess by midday. Weather with this kind of pattern, however, does promote getting the chores done early and quickly to allow time outside whilst the weather is good. Day by day, though, my motivation feels dampened by the weary weather.

I look over at my sewing pile, sigh. It is the same size pile that has been there for days. Probably more like weeks. I can't seem to concentrate or find any interest in the tasks I usually enjoy. I also find myself short of temper, and I feel lost in melancholiness. So, I sit by the window and look out, looking but not really seeing anything.

The slight breeze from this morning is becoming a chill wind. As I wrap my shawl more tightly around myself, I realize it's most likely a prudent idea to close my window shutter before depleting all the warmth from the room. Besides, I can smell the rain in the wind. We're in for another downpour tonight.

After closing up my chamber from the weather outside, I decide that maybe adding some brighter candlelight may help to elevate my mood and stave off the day's gloom. My mind wanders to the evening meal, maybe the harpist will play some lively music tonight. That should be welcomed by all! Weather like this puts most into a sour mood, either because of self-searching or intolerance to everything and everyone. A good meal, good company and lively music would certainly help cheer everyone.

The thought moves me to put on some brighter colors. The gown I have on is nice enough, but not much for inspiring me into a brighter mood. Maybe something in a vibrant green, with a floral pattern...yes, this one will do nicely!! After putting the new gown on, I check my appearance in the mirror. The dress fits nicely, not too snug but fitted enough to show off my figure, slight as it may be.

After giving myself approval on my gown, I move on to my hair. I think I should wear it pulled back, but not too severe. My skin is paler than I like with so little sunshine this Winter, but after adding a little crimson coloring to my lips, my face takes on a brighter appearance. I just needed to add my footwear for the evening and my look would be complete...these boots! I sit down on my footstool and begin lacing up my boots, and while carefully threading the laces, I find my thoughts drifting to my life here.

The evening meals were my favorite part of the day, I realize. Why? It is the time when we all come together to share a meal, a story, the warmth of the hearth fire, listen to music and sometimes even dance. There seemed to be an almost magical power of gratitude during this time when all of the day's grievances are forgiven. People sit at ease with one another and are thankful for the bounty we all worked together to create and share.

With boots laced, hair pulled up, lips dyed, I stand in front of my mirror for a final appraisal of my "look". On a girlish impulse, I spin around in front of my mirror, the rich folds of the gown swirling about my legs. I giggle despite myself. I take that for a good omen and leave my room, thinking tonight will indeed be better than today.

As Erenow heads down the castle hallway, towards the feasting hall. A stranger steps into her path. She greets the young man, wondering if he is lost. He returns her greeting and says that he is not lost and asks if he can accompany her on her way to the feasting hall. Erenow agrees, but she never makes it to the feasting hall, the stranger has different ideas.

Part 2

The waves crash far below where I sit. Sitting with my feet dangling precariously over the edge of the cliff...what would it feel like to fall?? The sky is clear and the wind is fierce, tearing at my hair and already torn gown. Through my teary eyes, looking out over the sea, I think I can see forever. All I need to do to reach it is to ease my body over the edge. I look down from where I sit. The waves seem almost peaceful so far below me. It feels strange to feel so calm, but the ocean always makes me feel so. Something about the way the waves crash up against the sand and rocks, then retreat back into itself, in the past, had always helped me solve my dilemmas. I am not sure now if my dilemma can be solved.

I had been attacked and beaten. I try not to think about all of it...but the pains in my body answer those questions. I am only thankful that I lost consciousness at some point, and when I awoke and found my clothing tattered and bloodied, and my body in a secluded corridor, I could only assume the worst. I didn't know if I had been left for dead, but I didn't wait to see if someone would come for me again. So I ran. I ran...and I ran. I ran toward where I had found solace and answers before...to the sea. I know the Castle Keep wasn't too far back in the distance...but I hoped I had run far enough for now. A seagull's cry above me brings me back to the cliff's edge.

How can I go back?? How can I trust anyone? People will talk, and I wouldn't know any response. But, if I didn't go back, where do I go??? How will I live??? My world has been shattered, and yet for all the despair I feel, my backside is firmly planted on the ground below me. A startling revelation comes to me, that yes I want to escape, but I don't want to be dead. I look out again at forever.... would I like living there??

Part 3

To the left of where the young girl is sitting on the cliff's edge is a glade of Cypress trees. Inside the glade, there is an inconspicuous onlooker.

This onlooker watches the young girl sitting on the cliffside with interest. She had been sitting for two days now without moving. The onlooker isn't sure if the girl had any concept of time or how she had stayed awake this long. Maybe this girl sleeps sitting up??

It seems that this poor creature had been through some harrowing experience by the look of her, so the onlooker, not wanting to create any more distress, keeps a discreet distance. Was this girl going to jump? The onlooker doesn't think so...they feel that this girl needs help...but wasn't sure of how to approach her safely.

The onlooker has never been in a situation like this before, and realizes that extreme care must be taken in approaching this girl.

The onlooker feels that this girl must fall asleep soon, so patience is employed, and the onlooker will wait her out. A rescue plan seems to form in their mind, which relies upon the girl falling asleep. Then the onlooker can carefully move the sleeping girl farther away from the cliff's edge and danger. The onlooker will be there when the girl awakens to reassure her that she is safe and will be cared for. A smile crosses the onlooker's face. This is a good plan. Having this decision firmly in mind, the onlooker gets comfortable and waits.

Part 4

The sun is lowering itself closer and closer to the ocean's cool embrace. The sky is brilliant with reds, oranges and vibrant yellows. The sky above, now vacant of the sun's presence, is different shades of blues fading to black. A black sky dotted with sparkling stars, and despite myself, I smile. It feels good to smile. I realize I am feeling something other than fear and dread and sadness. I realize I am so tired. Since I have decided that forever can wait, I slide my bottom and body back from the edge of the cliff, and I lay down on my side, using my arm for a pillow, and pull my legs in close for warmth. With the sun gone, the cold of night has arrived. The ground under me still held some warmth of the day, and as I lay there curled into a ball, I can feel myself relaxing and letting the sleep come.

The onlooker breathes a sigh of relief as they see the girl pull herself back away from the cliff's edge and then lay herself down for sleep. Once the onlooker is sure that the girl is asleep, the time has come to move her to safety. The girl is very slight, so lifting her is no hardship. With the girl in arms, the onlooker carries the girl into the safety of the Cypress grove.

Once inside the grove, the onlooker changes the plan and continues to carry the girl a bit farther to their cottage. At the cottage door, the onlooker pauses, still with the girl in arms. Before entering the cottage, there are recommended precautions that haven't been taken to protect this girl before entry. The onlooker senses the conflict inside their mind, but decides based on their heart instead. "What good are we as Guardians if we don't help?" With the question asked out loud, the Guardian answers themself and pushes through the door and enters the cottage.

The Guardian lays the girl down upon a bed. The cottage is a one-room structure. With the girl upon the bed, the Guardian finds a blanket to cover her and then awakens the fire. As the girl lays sleeping, the Guardian, with their mind, reaches out to the girl in her dreams to comfort her, but what she finds is the ordeal that this young girl has most recently faced. Because the Guardian hadn't prepared the girl, or themself, the Guardian is swept up in the trauma of it all.

........*so long I ran, through the brambles and brush, my gown torn, hair and skin torn and bloodied. Fear and shock drive me on now. The pursuit I feared never seemed to happen, but still fear drove me on. I can't stop. I could not rest. I feared I could not run fast enough or far enough to escape what was behind me. I no longer saw where I ran, or the obstacles in my path. But I could hear the waves. I could smell the sea. Go there, I told myself, GO THERE!*

The Guardian realizes what just happened and breaks the connection. At the same time, the girl sits straight up in confusion and disorientation in the bed.

"Where am I?" cries the girl.

Part 5

It is a time of beginnings and endings. It is my time of decision on which to follow. Sigh. The Guardian knows the fate of this girl and theirs is tied together now.

There is a slight shimmer in the room, and as the girl turns to look around her surroundings she sees a beautiful and well-dressed lady standing before her. This calms her and she asks again, in much calmer tones, "Where am I?"

"You are in my cottage in the Cypress Grove. You are safe here. My name is Aeolian, you can think of me as your guardian." Aeolian prided herself on telling the truth in an elusive way.

The young girl responds, "I am Erenow. I am grateful for your help and care."

Aeolian smiles warmly and genuinely at Erenow, and moves closer to help her lay down and re-covers her with the blanket. "You must sleep. You must rest. There will be time to talk later." And although these words didn't sound like a command, Erenow had no choice but to obey.

··●··

As Forbes is observing the story of Erenow, he senses this isn't a dream. At least not like the ones he's accustomed to. As he moves through this story, he has a sense that Aeolian knows he's there. She seems familiar somehow to him. And then, quite unexpectedly Aeolian looks directly at him, and smiles, acknowledging to him that he is correct.

··●··

Forbes awoke with a start. He sat straight up, and then felt the world spin around him. He must have cried out, because when the world stopped spinning, in front of him was the familiar face that steadied him. A wonderful, dirty, smelly face he now knew as home.

"Are you okay?" Greer asked. He just smiled his stupid smile that he did sometimes when she noticed him looking at her. She had no idea what it meant, but it made her uncomfortable, and she worried that he had been hit too hard. So she took hold of his shoulders, and asked him again, more slowly and deliberate, "Are you okay?" She was trying to make sure he was comprehending her question.

Her closeness, her touch...

He answered her, "Yes." Then, his memory came back, and he asked her the same question with an urgency that seemed out of place, "Are you okay?" And then he frantically searched the camp for their attacker.

His question irritated her. Of course, she's alright, wasn't she the one caring for him? He noted her irritation and once more realized he understood so little about his companion.

While he was unconscious...

Greer had been fretting all night. She hated fretting. But, she was a bit off her game—one man tied up and bagged and another unconscious and with a head wound. She guessed, rightly so, that this was a fret-worthy situation. With nothing to do and needing to stay alert, she had an idea.

She moved to the back of her cart and looked for a special sack. It's the one that Carter and her would keep all the extra bits of fabric to be repurposed. She sorted through the many kinds of fabric until she found what she wanted. Next, she searched for the special wooden box that contained the tools for sewing. She had had an idea brewing in her mind and working on this would keep her alert and awake.

So armed with her choice of fabric bits and the sewing kit, she returned to the fire. She looked over at Forbes, who was still unconscious, but breathing well. His pulse had felt strong and normal when she last checked it. She relaxed a little.

Putting her work down by her on a flat rock, which she used both as a table and a seat, she went over to check on the boy. She didn't get too close, but he seemed like he was alive. She could see his body rise and fall with his breaths. She would wait for daylight before she did anything else with him, and she hoped Forbes would be awake and back to himself soon.

She sat close enough to the fire for light, but not too close because too much heat would make her drowsy. The warmth of her dung fire always comforted her. She looked over to her dozing cow, and was once more so thankful for Jow, her animal companion.

She laid out a little scrap about the size of her two hands onto her lap. She glanced over at Forbes lying under his worn blanket, and smiled. He'd only been part of her life for a short while, and she recognized now that he was important to her. The stories he told her were only part of the reason. She wasn't really ready to think about any other reasons, because she was so unsure of what she did feel. But, even so, she wanted to do something for him, and his blanket did need some repairing.

She took a moment to stare into the flames without really seeing them, and thought about the first story he had shared with her after they met, about Meridal and her golden arrow. And then with a smile widening across her face, she had her idea firmly in her mind.

Next, she picked up the wooden box that contained the sewing tools and thread, and found a thick yellow thread that would do nicely. She had in her lap a dark green fabric, which was the color she imagined a forest in England would be. She carefully stitched an outline of an arrow with four roses.

She continued with her work till sunrise.

CHAPTER 8

The Meaning of Trust

Now that Forbes was truly awake, and knew that Greer was indeed "okay," his curiosity finally got the better of him. It was obvious to him she wasn't going to tell him on her own, so he asked. "Well, what did you do with him?"

Greer was bent over her cooking pot, stirring their breakfast. She gave one last stir, tapped the spoon and then put it down on a plate. She moved closer to Forbes so their voices would be lower. He was very alert now. She nodded her head twice to her left, so he looked there. He was quite impressed with what he saw, so he smiled and looked back at her.

"After you brained him with the rock, and I knew you were mostly ok, I tied him up like Carter showed me. He hasn't moved much, but he is breathing steadily. I haven't gotten too close. I am not sure if he's still out or playing it that way. I wanted you to be with me when I checked, you know, the two are better than one strategy," she finished speaking very softly.

Forbes felt very good about her considering him an asset in battle. Yesterday, he wouldn't have guessed she felt that way. She pretty much knocked him down over and over during their "training." His head still felt a little foggy, so he wasn't up quite yet for another go around with anyone. So, he looked at her and whispered back, "Well, looks like you have things well in hand... so let's eat breakfast first, then check on him."

Greer appreciated his positive comments, but also realized he had just gotten himself out of morning meal duty.

As they ate in relative silence, their captive peered at them through the burlap sack which was over his head while laying still. He was quite unsure of what would happen next, and he was surprised to find that he was enjoying himself. He rarely had this kind of time to himself. He spent most of his days following the instructions of others. His days were very predictable...this day was not. He didn't have to wait too long to find out what would happen next.

After the meal was complete, the campsite was all tidied up as if they were getting ready to depart. The Storyteller came close enough to give him a little kick, to which he instinctively responded, "Hey!"

Forbes bent down, and helped their captive up into a sitting position, then using his knife, cut an opening into the sack and pulled it down around his shoulders. He heard Greer groan, knowing he'd be getting a sewing lesson next.

Then Forbes, knife still in hand, moved back away and sat on a rock facing their captive. Now that their captive no longer pretended to be asleep, he all of a sudden realized he was hungry and needed to relieve himself and he was thirsty. Greer noticed the squirm, and using her gruff voice said, "He won't talk until he takes care of something." Forbes nodded in agreement.

Greer tossed a fighting staff to Forbes and moved in to untie the rope so Forbes wouldn't cut it. The youth stood up with some assistance from Greer, who appeared much stronger than he had supposed, as Forbes prodded him off a ways to relieve himself. The sack was still around his shoulders and arms, but he could use his hands a little.

Afterwards, he was ushered back to the campsite, instructed to sit, and Greer re-tied his hands and feet. Then he sat facing the Storyteller and the Carter named Greer.

"Why did you attack us?" Forbes got straight to the point. Then, Forbes realized he had never bothered to get the youth's name when he was his attendant. And so he asked another question before the youth could answer the first, "What do they call you?"

The youth looked at them both, the Storyteller first, then the Carter Greer, then the Storyteller again, and answered with a question of his own, "Why did you leave?"

Forbes thought on this question for a moment, and then in an instant felt brilliant and said, "This merchant Carter offered me a contract in a distant village. Since I had already fulfilled my duties to your community, I was free to accept. We left right away because the distance we need to travel is great. Vast, one might even say."

The youth's eyes switched over to the Carter Greer, and his eyes narrowed as he tried to sense the validity of the Storyteller's words. It was as if the Carter's face was made of stone, giving nothing away.

Greer thought to herself, Forbes is masterful. Forbes thought to himself, we could make a lot of money playing cards.

The youth had seemed to weigh his options, and telling the truth seemed in order.

"My name is Kairos. My masters believed that your leaving so abruptly was due to some fault in my task of attending to you. They wanted another story from you. They sent me after you, after the four they sent after you first returned in worse condition than when they departed," the youth offered up.

Greer couldn't stand it anymore, she had to ask, "Why, if your masters so appreciated the skill of this Storyteller, would they send ruffians after him?" She finished asking her question with her hands in fists anchored at her waist. The youth felt the Carter looked very formidable, and Forbes knew the youth's instincts were right.

Kairos answered right away, "Well, I thought maybe you had kidnapped him," he blurted out.

"Oh," so Greer continued in outrage, "so, because you felt threatened and feared retribution you sent ruffians upon us, and then when they failed their attack on us, you attacked us when you found us?"

Forbes wanted to calm her down so she wouldn't give away anything they didn't want known. "Well, Kairos," Forbes said smoothly, "I have not been kidnapped. I am not in danger, at least not anymore," he finished, rubbing his head a bit from where Kairos had struck him last night. "We'll give you a bit of food and water and send you on your way back," Forbes finished. Greer had kept her eyes on him while Forbes spoke, and noticed that the youth was squirming now, she supposed, for a more complicated reason.

Greer spoke again, this time measured and calm, but the edge in her voice was distinct, "You were told not to return unless the Storyteller was with you. And if you don't return, they will send others, and if you return with him they will still send others." She kept her eyes on Kairos' face as did Forbes. He shook his head in response. Yes.

Greer stood there with her hands on her hips, looking like a storm cloud ready to explode in fury.

Forbes held his breath.

"Oh cut him loose," she said. "He'll come with us. Three warriors are better than two." Just like that, Greer had decided his purpose. Kairos didn't know anything about her really, or about Forbes' ability with dimension dreaming and story trinket souvenirs. And, it would prove a good test of the disguise her father Carter had worked so hard upon creating. She knew without a doubt that Forbes would never betray her.

"I'll work on caring for Jow, while you get him something to eat," Greer finished and she moved to her task of caring for the cow.

Forbes, a bit bewildered, followed her instructions at once. Kairos was thrilled to be having a breakfast he didn't cook, and that he was about to have an adventure.

CHAPTER 9

What is Love?

G reer had always lived with a man. Her father, after all, was a man. She didn't expect it to feel so different with other men. Now, despite her usual aversion to crowds, she seemed to be collecting men!

She had been fine with Forbes. He was interesting. He told her stories. She was training him in things he had never learned or done for himself. He made her feel important somehow. But now, this boy! Sigh. She did feel that he'd do better with them than back where he had come from. She wasn't sure how much Kairos really was grasping, but by the excitement in his response, she knew he welcomed a different kind of adventure to the task he had been sent upon.

Greer was honestly just learning how to be Greer without her father. She felt she could relax and be herself with Forbes...but, now she needed to be extra cautious. Not forgetting that her life and Forbes' depended on others believing she was a male.

She had figured that growing up with her father, every man had similar skill sets. Forbes had cleared that up. And now, this boy. He'd need evaluating, but she believed he'd be capable of following instructions. Hopefully, cooking would be one of his learned skills. She missed the type of meals her father would make on occasion when they had either hunted/fished or bartered for supplies.

So, with her cart packed, Jow fed and hitched up, the makeshift campsite restored to look natural and undisturbed by campers,

Greer set off on their road with Forbes and Kairos following. Forbes let Kairos know that the pace would be brisk and even, but there would be rests. Forbes figured correctly that today would be a walk-in-silence-kinda-day while Greer ran over things in her head. Forbes also guessed correctly that getting as far away as possible from trackers was imperative. He kept Kairos in front of him to make sure that the boy wasn't doing anything to leave tracks for any would-be followers. Forbes questioned his eagerness to join them as well as the boy's loyalties.

Kairos lost his enthusiastic smile at a new adventure after about four hours of non-stop walking and no talking. He felt like his brain was numb and his legs just moved in rhythm to the sound of the cow's harness and cartwheels. Where were they going, and would they ever get there???

The sun in the sky seemed to have already reached its main height and was already starting its downward decline before they stopped. Kairos was so hungry that his stomach growled at him. Even on the busiest of days, he and the other workers were given regular meal breaks.

But Forbes' words rang true, and they did come to a stop once the Carter had found a secluded spot for the cart, cow and themselves to rest, out of the view of anyone. Kairos thought to himself, who would ever walk this far into nowhere? But he was grateful for the rest. And plopped himself onto the ground unceremoniously in exhaustion with a loud sigh.

Greer looked over at him, and she scowled a bit, then breathed out a long sigh as well, for a different kind of exhaustion. She wondered to herself about this boy's fitness; she had supposed he would be more fit.

Forbes watched the exchange with a little chuckle to himself, glad that someone else's fitness for long travel days irked Greer rather than his own. Actually, now that he thought about it, he wasn't tired or winded. That thought surprised him.

As much as Forbes observed Greer, Greer observed Forbes. She saw his little chuckle, guessed rightly what it was about, and then noticed Forbes standing a bit taller. And now she chuckled to herself. But she was happy to see Forbes happy, and proving to be a good learner and traveling companion.

Forbes moved closer to Greer, not wanting the boy to overhear every conversation.

"What are the plans?" he asked conspiratorially.

Greer looked at him, looked at Kairos sitting exhausted in the dirt, looked down at her own feet, and then back to Forbes.

"We need a meal. I'm not sure about anything else. If someone is trailing the boy, they may have a faster mode of travel than us. I think we will eat, rest in the daylight, and then move on again through the night. The weather seems clear so the moon will give us some help in moving on," she answered.

She didn't know what she expected Forbes' response to be, so she found herself surprised when he seemed in perfect agreement. And even more surprised when he said, "Okay then, you go relieve yourself first. Then take care of Jow, and I'll see to the fire and the food with Kairos."

Not wanting to appear to not have a united front, Greer agreed and walked a ways off by herself.

When she returned, she was alone except for Jow, who looked at her, hoping for water and a meal as well.

She looked at Jow and asked, "Where did they go?" Jow just shook her head, and resettled her harness.

"Hmph," Greer responded to Jow's non-verbal response, "you don't know either?" Greer moved to get some water for Jow and then put her ration into a bucket, placing the bucket in front of the cow on the ground. Greer then stood in front of Jow, gently stroking the cow's head, absently lost in her own thoughts. The cow enjoyed the attention.

Greer assumed that Forbes wouldn't have let Kairos go off on his own for any relieving, and was making sure that he didn't run off or catch them off guard again. Her thoughts of late always seemed to come back to Forbes. It must be because he was new in her world, but a part of her felt like maybe it was something more. What it could be, she couldn't guess. And then, she realized all of a sudden that she was happy. She felt happy! She hadn't felt happy since her father died. She felt happy like when she and her father were together. And with that thought came another feeling, a swell in her heart at the realization that she was happy because of Forbes. Not just because he meant companionship and someone to share a meal and burdens of the day with, but because she felt love for him like she had felt love for her father. But the love she realized she felt for Forbes felt different.

The love she felt for her father was full of gratitude and safety and trust. The love she realized she was feeling for Forbes was full of...more. After a moment of realizing this feeling of love, she felt lighter than air. She closed her eyes. She could feel herself smiling. All of her felt alive and bristling with energy. She felt almost as if she glowed, and then she remembered that love only leads to pain. She had loved her father, and then he was gone. She was alone. She thought of Forbes, and what if he died like her father, or worse, he tired of their travels together and preferred to return to his storytelling without her. Then, almost as fast as the lightness had arrived, it was crushed by a wave of fear of loss and loneliness. She couldn't breathe. Her throat shut. She could feel her heart beating erratically. And then darkness consumed her as she fell to the ground beside her cow.

Forbes and Kairos had walked off a bit from the camp, although they still kept to the shrubbery. Kairos was thankful for the respite because he very badly needed to "relieve" himself. At least that was what Forbes had said they were going to do. Kairos had thought once or twice about running back to the relative safety of his hamlet, but he realized he'd only be punished for failing in his task, and thought taking his chances with a credited Storyteller and a Carter seemed a better option.

Forbes took care of himself as well, having faith that the boy wouldn't run away before a meal at least. He couldn't rightly say that he was happy for the additional person in their adventure. He was rather enjoying himself with Greer, more than any other time in his life that he could remember. He was totally out of his element, and yet felt totally happy. Happy. No, not just happy. Elated! He had never really had a friend, at least not one he had spent nearly this amount of concentrated time with, and never with one quite as interesting.

Friend. Friend? Is that what Greer had become to him? He thought about his other friends, whom he didn't miss at all. He didn't want to be away from Greer. He actually realized he wasn't even excited about sharing her with Kairos. He wanted and enjoyed being alone with her. He wanted to protect her. He wanted her to trust and rely on him. He wanted to be more than her friend. But what did that even mean?

He thought about the stories he told, and the characters in those stories, those dreams. He didn't know about love personally, but he had experienced what it felt like through those dreams. If he were a character in one of his dreams, he now understood he would be in the midst of falling in love. He was falling in love with Greer, that both made him smile like an idiot and catch his stomach wrenching in fear.

Which was pretty much when Kairos walked back over to him, "What happened to you?"

Forbes looked at Kairos, and answered, "Huh?" Then he removed his hands from his stomach, stood up straight and gave his whole self a good shake and said, "It's nothing, just shaking to get the travel dust off."

Kairos said, "Oh good idea." And then proceeded to shake his whole self as well.

Forbes rolled his eyes at him, and then said, "C'mon."

Kairos fell in step with Forbes. He was very nearly as tall as him but not nearly as solid. Kairos was in the mood for some conversation after such a long and quiet morning into the late afternoon of walking. "Do you know where we are going?"

Forbes answered cautiously, "The Carter has a destination in mind which I agreed to."

"Hmph. So is the Carter Greer, the Greer from your story? And if so, does that make him a him or not?"

Forbes decided to pull a little rank, "Storytellers do not divulge how they create their stories or why."

"Hmph." But Kairos had more questions that he never got to ask, because as the two of them neared their camp, Forbes could hear Jow mooing in a distressed tone, and he took off running. Kairos followed close behind and could see Greer collapsed beside the cow.

She was crumpled on the ground. Forbes did a quick scan and didn't see anyone else there. The cow was looking at him, so he asked the cow, "What happened?" To which the cow mooed even louder.

He moved quickly to her body and he could see she was breathing. "Greer?" He said her name, unsure of whether he should touch her since he didn't know why she was lying there in the first place. He looked around again for a possible attacker, and didn't see anything out of the ordinary other than Greer.

Kairos looked around as well, not wanting to get brained again since he'd only just recovered.

Forbes risked shaking her a bit, "Greer?" Then he asked a bit more insistently with both his words and shaking, "Greer, wake up!"

He leaned over her again to make sure she was still breathing at the same time that she sat up with the force of a bolt. She smacked Forbes' forehead with the top of her head.

"Agh!!" He yelled out in pain as he held his hand to his forehead with blood running through his fingers and then down his face.

"What are you doing?" she growled at him. "What happened?"

"Ow, that hurt!" he answered, sitting back, still holding his head. "I don't know," he continued, "You were laying there in a crumpled heap beside the cow. The cow was mooing loudly so we ran into camp and found you. I was checking to see if you were alive," he finished, equally combative.

"Well," she answered with less sternness in her voice, "I'm obviously not dead."

"No, you're not. Not even wounded." And then he reached over and took the cow's water and began washing the blood from his hand and face. Greer recovered from her shock and anger, moved quickly to the back of the cart to get a cloth to help clean the wound and stop the bleeding. She felt self-conscious tending to him with Kairos just standing there watching all of this. So she put the rag into Forbes' hand and told him to apply pressure. Then she stood up, patted the cow, and moved again to the back of the cart.

"Kairos, time to make yourself useful."

Kairos, who had simply stood there observing the whole scene, shook his head in agreement. What a strange day.

The first step in getting Kairos up to speed was to instruct him on how to choose the pieces of dung that were ready to burn. To her surprise, he didn't show the same aversion to this task that Forbes had originally. She guessed he most likely had helped in the stables from time to time. The next step was showing him how to measure out the water into the appropriate cooking container, and then setting up the cooking tripod from which the cooking container would be suspended over the small but warm fire.

He took to the work willingly and with ease. Greer breathed a sigh of relief for small favors. Her self-consciousness had faded a bit, but she didn't like being so close in proximity to him. Curious. Was it fear or personal preference?

With Kairos fully engaged now in the cooking process, she returned to see what tending Forbes would need for his newest head wound.

Forbes had been sitting there dutifully holding the wet rag hard against his head wound, all the while watching how Greer went about acclimating and instructing their newest camp addition to life on the road. He was amazed once again by her efficiency and clarity of instruction which allowed Kairos (whom obviously had much more training and familiarity with this sort of stuff) to work on his own very quickly. Forbes was glad for this for more than the obvious reason, not just because he didn't have to do it himself, but because his head hurt and his arm was straining to keep the pressure on his wound. He was quite happy that it was now his turn to have Greer's attention.

"How's it feeling?" Greer asked, keeping her voice low and as free of emotion as possible.

"I think the bleeding has stopped," was his response.

She sighed in relief in a direction only he could see. "Well, let me have a look at it and see what needs to be done. Sit farther back against the wagon wheel for support, just in case." Forbes followed her instructions and scooched himself along the dirt, still holding the rag until his back was firmly against the wagon wheel. Then he dropped his hand slowly, expecting the rag to come away with his hand but it stayed firmly attached to his forehead.

Greer noticed this and sort of scrunched up her face in an expression of consternation. She looked at him and said, "I'll be right back." She got herself up out of her crouch and moved past Kairos working on their meal to the back of the cart again looking for her sewing kit and some herbs her Father and her had dried and stored for wounds that were a bit more serious. With her kit and herbs, she moved back to Forbes. She put her items down and Jow mooed a bit. She got back up and moved to Jow.

"He took your water didn't he? Hmm, well let's get you some more." And the cow stomped her back feet a bit and shook her head, to which Greer responded, "Okay, it's a walk you need first."

Kairos was astonished, the Carter was having a conversation with the cow. He'd been around animals and caretakers, but he'd never seen this before. Greer looked over at him and asked, "Kairos, would you please take Jow for a short walk away from our camp to relieve herself? And remember where she leaves things so we can retrieve them later." Kairos shook his head in agreement, put down his cooking implements and took hold of the cow's reins. Again, he thought, what a strange day.

As he moved off with Jow, and Greer was sure he was out of earshot, she squatted down in front of Forbes once more. Forbes recognized her sewing kit, saw the herbs, and figured rightly that this was going to hurt more than it did already. But he also understood it had to be taken care of. Greer knew this was going to hurt from her own past experiences of growing up. Her father would always distract her with conversation. She thought she would employ the same tactic.

"This might hurt a bit as I pull off the rag that helped with the clotting. I'm going to pull slowly to try and preserve the seal it created. Once off, I am going to clean just a bit more to see if I need to sew you back together."

Forbes kept his eyes on her face, and on her eyes, when she looked at his. On her lips, when she spoke with her eyes focused on his wound. She was so dirty, and smelly, and yet everything about her made him feel alive.

"Okay," she continued, "it's not as bad as it could've been. It'll just take two tiny stitches." And then she stopped talking, and kinda started humming as she threaded the needle and very carefully threaded it through his skin. She tied off almost as soon as she had started. Then she gave a small amount of dried herbs to him to chew lightly and spit back into her hand. She then pressed the herb/spit paste into the wound on his forehead. Lastly, she took a long strip of cleanish linen and tied it around his head. "This will keep the paste where I want it." Forbes tried to nod in agreement, but that made his head spin a little.

Kairos and Jow hadn't made their way back, so Greer asked Forbes, "Why were you leaning over me?" She tried to ask in a nonchalant manner, trying not to give away her invested interest in his answer.

"Well," he started, "I could see you were breathing, but when you didn't respond to your name or my voice, I wanted to make sure you were really breathing." His answer made her smile. He realized how much he liked it when she smiled.

"Thank you for checking on me and for your concern," she answered. Forbes thought he heard a softness in her voice he had never heard before. Greer turned her head in a listening pose, noticing that Kairos and the cow were on their way back. Her demeanor changed instantly as did the character of her voice. "You sit back and rest while Kairos and I finish preparing the meal. We have more traveling to do yet today."

And with that Greer gathered her sewing kit and healing supplies, and returned them back into the cart. She greeted Kairos as he returned, and complimented his work. "You continue with the meal making for us, and I'll get Jow's oats prepared." Kairos agreed, returned to his meal-making, observing the newly bandaged Forbes, and thinking he was fortunate to be with the Carter and Storyteller.

Since Forbes wasn't good for much right now, he revisited his thoughts from earlier about his feelings and Greer. The first thought that came to him was through his sense of smell as there was a slight breeze shift and the dung smoke blew straight at him. He breathed in the smell, as one would expect to do with a lovely flower. It struck him that not only did he not mind the smell, but the smell itself meant home. It meant Greer.

He watched her and Kairos working together to care for Jow, and prepare the meal and he thought it looked like a well-rehearsed team. But didn't he just join them?? Kairos seemed genuinely happy with this new change in his life. And seeing that in someone else made him realize that he was genuinely happy with this change in his own life.

He thought about his life as a Storyteller. About the stories he told, and realized he might someday be a character in some other storyteller's tale. He thought about what his stories were about at their core. He was surprised to think that they were all about love. But, what did he know about love? He didn't know if he himself had actually ever felt love other than through the characters in his dreams. He did actually feel what they felt. So then, he surmised, that he did know about romantic love, family love, love of self and love gone wrong. His storied dreams had taught him about loss, sacrifice, compassion, fear, hope, joy and triumph.

So if he had experienced these feelings through his characters, he should be able to sense his own. What did he feel? Why had he followed her? Mere curiosity, or a longing of his own? He knew he felt happy, even now sitting here, leaned up against a wagon wheel in the dirt with a throbbing head watching a character from his dream story come to life. She was real. This moment was real. He felt as if he belonged in a way he had never before. Not just accepted, and applauded, but a real belonging. He felt open, with a willingness and a curiosity he imagined he felt as a child learning his trade. He also felt hungry.

And as he looked over to see if the meal was near completion and on its way over to him, he realized he had a deeper hunger. His focus sharpened on Greer and she was looking straight at him with a puzzled look on her face. She spooned out his portion into a crudely made wooden bowl and handed it back to Kairos to deliver to Forbes. Then she spooned out her own portion and moved a bit away from the fire to eat. Forbes felt his face flush with embarrassment at showing something to her he hadn't meant to, and worried he had frightened her somehow. What did he know of love?

After eating his meal, Forbes felt more relaxed than he had in days. The daylight was still in the sky, and he figured his body needed to recover so he let himself drift off to sleep once he had put his bowl down next to him.

Kairos and Greer also finished their meals. And Greer had one more important lesson for Kairos before she would allow him to rest as well. Cleaning up. Leave no trace. And retrieving the dung from earlier to dry a bit near the now dwindling fire. Greer had to smile that Kairos was such a keen student. And of course Kairos noticed the smile, and asked, "Carter, why are you smiling?"

His voice caught her off guard, but she responded, still smiling, "Because you are such a fast learner. And I was thinking about how much I enjoyed learning from my father." Then his next question really threw her off her game.

"Carter, is it true you're a female?"

Greer tried to mask her surprise at the question, moderated her vocal tone to steady and low tones and then responded, "Kairos, we don't need stations out here in the nowhere. You can call me Greer. And, do I look like a female to you??" She actually dared him to look at her, which Kairos did up and down. Then, with a kind of disappointed head shake and sideways mouth grimace expressing his disappointment, he said, "No, I guess not. You're not as smelly as some other men I've known, but you're pretty close. Why would the storyteller say you were?" He asked in his youthful confusion.

Greer merely shrugged and responded, "Well, he's a storyteller and he has to keep his audience entertained." Kairos found that the most suitable answer and much more believable than that this Carter person was a female.

With all that out of the way, Kairos felt more comfortable asking questions about where they were going, what was next, and whether he would be trained in healing wounds as well. Greer chuckled a camaraderie kind of chuckle and said, "Well, I think those questions can wait. We'll be traveling as soon as dusk begins, so rest up." Kairos didn't need to be asked twice. He leaned up next to the back wagon wheel since Forbes was leaning on the front one and relaxed into sleep.

Greer made use of the remaining daylight, not feeling tired, by pulling out her secret sewing project, and continuing her work on her story quilt squares.

The time passed quickly, and she had her project stored away before she moved to wake up Forbes. He woke up quickly, and then relaxed after Greer merely pointed out it was time to get started again. She knew he'd take a bit of extra time to get himself ready. He seemed more steady to her after his rest. Next, she moved to wake up Kairos. He took a little more jostling, but then finally roused. "Go take care of yourself, we're leaving now."

Still sort of groggy, he confirmed, "You mean relieve myself?" Greer shook her head in affirmative.

As he was leaving, Forbes returned and helped Greer with any last-minute tie-ups to make sure the camp was cleared of their time there as much as possible. Forbes assured her he felt much better and although feeling silly about the head wrap, was ready to go. Kairos learned that Greer was true to her words and as Dusk fell, they departed.

CHAPTER 10

Uncharted Moment

They had started out at a pretty good pace. And Greer had predicted the weather correctly. It was clear and the full moon did provide a good deal of light for them. Forbes had noticed that the area they were traveling through seemed particularly sparse of natural wildlife. "Greer, don't you think it's odd that there is such a lack of wildlife and the sounds they make?" he asked.

And Kairos echoed, "Yeah, I was noticing that too."

Greer cocked her head a bit with her right ear raised, and said, "Yes, but it has always been so in here. And I guess my Father and I lived here for so many seasons that the lack of sounds here always felt like coming home."

"Do you have a specific destination for tonight?" Forbes changed the subject.

"Yes."

"Care to elaborate?"

"No."

And so, Forbes left it at that. Kairos chuckled to himself. They were an interesting pair to be around.

And as they walked, Greer thought to herself, I do know where we are headed. She felt guilty not sharing, but she wasn't sure she could find it. Her father had once told her of a great body of water he called an ocean. She wanted to see it for herself. She also thought it would be so far away from wherever she had been before that no one would ask questions. Except for Forbes. And, definitely Kairos.

So as Greer was lost in her own thoughts, Forbes also rummaged through his. He was surprised he had not dimension dreamt but was also relieved because he really did feel better. More refreshed and clear headed. So he ruminated on his last dream-like event about Erenow and Aeolian. Did he just imagine she looked at him?? And almost as immediately as he thought it, he heard a voice in his head that was not his own say "*No.*"

He stopped short in his tracks, which of course stopped Greer in hers which of course caused Kairos to walk smack into the back of the cart and knock himself out. The thud of a falling body was an unwelcome sound. Greer ran to the back of the cart. And as she suspected, there lay the unconscious body of Kairos. Forbes showed up just behind her and asked, "How did this happen?"

A very quick glance showed that the extra fighting poles were jutting out from the top layer of the cart. Even in the moonlight-filled darkness, they were easy to miss. So to answer Forbes' question, she replied, "Bad luck."

"What do we do?"

"Well, we aren't going to leave him. He's very useful. And he seemed to be enjoying himself. Well, at least until he knocked himself out."

"We need to keep going."

"Yes, we do. Can you shift some items on the cart bed to make it flat enough to lay him in?" Greer asked. She was checking Kairos out. "There's no blood, and he's breathing fairly normal. He does have a big egg-shaped bump on his forehead though."

Forbes got to work on making space for him besides the cart's contents. Then to his surprise, Greer reached down and very adeptly picked the youth up and placed him into the cart. Forbes was astonished at her strength. And then wondered why anything she did astonished him. She laid him down so gently, and then used her own blanket to cover him and then some rope to tie him in. Then she had Forbes help her, using the fighting staffs, to create a sturdy barrier to hold the other cart contents from shifting onto Kairos as he recovered while they continued to travel.

When she was sure the contents were secure, and that no more mishaps would occur, she leaned on the cart and sighed from her efforts. Forbes sighed too. She was standing so close to him, so very close. Even in the moonlight, Forbes could see all the dirt and grime she had purposefully left on her skin to cover her age and sex, but even so, this close, there were glimpses of skin. Her perfect skin. And he could smell her, all the soot and smoke from the dung fire and sweat from honest work, and he believed he'd never smelt anything so good. He closed his eyes and took a deep breath.

Greer didn't remember ever standing this close to him before without him being wounded. She felt funny inside. She sort of felt funny since she had met him. She didn't understand the funny-ness, but she wanted to do something to make it stop. She felt unsure and wary and happy and, well, all these sorts of feelings all jumbled up inside of her. He was so close, she could feel his body heat. She thought maybe she could hear his heartbeat too, until she realized it was her own pounding inside her ears.

Something was happening. His eyes were closed now. What had we been talking about? Forbes opened his eyes and there was Greer looking at him. What he did next, he would never know exactly why, but he did it.

He reached down and encircled Greer into his arms and squarely planted his mouth on hers for a kiss.

There was an explosion of energy. Every part of Greer felt on fire and tingling, but there was no burning, only light. She grabbed onto Forbes, fearing he would let go of her. She never wanted him to let go of her again. And as she grabbed onto him, she could feel him grab more tightly onto her.

Forbes felt a hunger he'd never realized he'd hungered for; this kiss, he never wanted it to end. He felt whole for the very first time in his life. Every part of him felt alive and vibrating. Then Forbes felt it - the shift, the dreaming was coming on him and he worried he'd crush her in his fall.

Greer felt she couldn't breathe. Her legs felt weak and seemed to be failing her. An overwhelming sense of sleep was overtaking her. She felt Forbes' body moving downward toward the ground, bringing her with him. She clung to him and could feel his arms still around her as they slid to the ground. Then she knew only sleep.

Forbes could feel her body limp in his arms. How could this be happening to her? And, as he got them both safely to the ground on the side of the cart, he had no more time to ask questions before the dream-story engulfed both of them.

Opalessence

—— ·•●•· ——

Energy! Flurries of it! Surging! Pulsing!
I AM ALIVE!
I stretch out my arms wide, face turned towards the full moon, "I am alive and well. Thank You." I bow in appreciation to the moon, then continue spinning round and round in a gleeful dance. I laugh and hug myself, falling to the ground, finally out of breath!

It has been a long time since I last danced so energetically. I have been gone for so long...too long. The incredible part of it is that I know I have been gone, but I don't know where I had gone to. I had not felt alive, but I knew I wasn't eternally dead.

Right now, here, free and alive, I didn't care to know. I am happy. I smile as I lay upon the damp grass beneath my body. The flowers are all sleeping for the night. The tall and sturdy oaks stand above me in their enduring way. Farther off I can smell the salty ocean. Senses! To have them back...to experience it all!! I stand up and run towards the smell of the ocean and the sound of the breakers crashing upon the sand. I must see.

As she runs off towards the waiting ocean, a figure steps from a shadow to watch her. So beautiful, so free. How could anyone have imprisoned such a spirit??? She knows nothing of the experience; remembers nothing. Remarkable!

A worried furrow crosses the brow of the watching figure. How long will it be before her freedom is discovered? Not long enough to be sure. Time, never enough time. As her figure moves farther away and becomes a dark blot on the horizon, the watching figure moves to follow her.

Splashing!! What a sensation! Cold, sparkling water, I think, "I'll call it 'the salt of life'." Completely drenched now, I realize the chill of the breeze. It makes me shiver. Oooh, I don't like it. "I don't like you," I say defiantly to the small, barely noticeable but defiant presence of the breeze.

Turning my back on the unfriendly breeze, I run off to find a soft, secluded patch of grass and flowers back within the safety of the oaks and fellow trees.

As the watching figure cautiously reappears, she is sleeping like a newborn child upon the soft grass with only the light of the moon blanketing her. A gentle warm breeze now blows over her, drawing a deep breath to savor its sweetness. The figure suddenly grows tense. Wrong, all wrong. Shivers run over both their bodies, the watcher and the sleeper. How could protection be offered? She will not accept or understand. Turmoil pulling the watching figure's mind far from decision, at least any coherent ones.

A strong wind now whips up and batters at the body watching her, pushing the watcher away. A furious gale wind begins forming a wall. The watcher feels panic. Panic! She is so unaware of her danger! The watcher grabs at an oak's trunk...I must not leave her. I must hold. Just as the wind has forced the watcher's body into the air and had almost wrenched the watcher's grip from the tree...the wind stops. The watcher falls onto the unyielding ground. A warning?? Yes, it must be. Running back to the previous spot prior to the wind force to check on her, fearing she would not be there. A deep breath...but she is. She lay still sleeping, unaffected. She is so precious.

But then the watcher looks again...and her countenance even in sleep has changed, just a subtle difference. But a detectable one. The sleeping smile she had before is now somehow saddened?? The watcher's shoulders sink a little, leaning into the tree that provided cover...her face now reveals the look of lost innocence. When she awakens from her slumber...the world will be changed for her.

But this change, though meant to harm her, could mean that now she will understand and possibly accept the protection being offered. The watching figure moves from the shadows into the glade where she sleeps—sitting down beside her, waiting, waiting for her to awaken.

The dawn breaks slowly, letting Sister Moon fall peacefully to sleep while Brother Sun awakens the world. Mornings hold such beauty. Light creation. The stirring of life. Life!! She begins to stir...she too is awakening. Doubts arise inside of the watcher. Will she accept me? Will she accept my reasons? She stretches herself languidly, as a cat would from a nap. She is so beautiful. And then the watcher knows that she knows she is being watched and that she is no longer alone.

Without turning I can feel the presence of another near me. Another being like myself?? Shall I turn around?? Or, shall I simply get up and walk away, pretending not to notice their presence? No, what have I to fear? Vaguely I remember having a bad dream, but it isn't clear. I feel no menace here, so I turn around.

Besides me sits a beautiful man. His whole being exudes calm beauty, inner peace. I know him for a friend at once. He is darker than myself, both skin and hair. His hair, though dark, has fiery highlights of red and gold. The wave of his hair causes the colors to shift as he moves. His eyes are green, like the deep green of the forest...and inside the color...passion! Such passion, it takes my breath. I must be smiling at him for he bows a welcome to me. Then he addresses me as if I am royalty.

"My Lady, one so fair as you should not travel these woods alone. I would be quite honored if you would allow me to escort you to your destination." As he speaks to me all I hear is music.

Breathe. I close my eyes to focus. Then, reopening them, I address him in kind, "Kind Sir, I would be most appreciative to have an escort so noble as yourself." Then I continue, "But, I have no known destination since I am only just this past night, alive." I watch his face, not sure of how my plain speak will be interpreted.

But his face shows no sign of startlement, rather his face shows only relief.

She has accepted me!

Smiling at her, she smiles back. Then in the forest, songbirds fill the air with song as if they are echoing his joy. He stands, bent over, and offers her a hand, which she accepts, and then he draws her up from her grassy bed to stand with him.

As he stands, I draw in my breath. He is pure splendor! A finely wrought man with the presence of a king. I gladly take the hand he offers to me. A decision I will never regret.

She is so trusting, so gentle, so fragile. Her spirit shines in so many colors, he can almost see them through her milky skin. Eyes so bright - so fiery. Her amber-red hair falls in gentle waves over her shoulders and down her back. She wears only a white gown of velvet, but it shimmers as she moves. A queen! This beautiful, young creature should be a queen. He will see to her safety and see her fulfill her destiny. (Whilst unknowingly fulfilling his own.)

"The day is just born, are you hungry?" her escort asks her politely.

I have to think. I don't remember hungry. So I answer honestly, "I don't know hungry."

"Well," he continues, "it's an empty feeling you get here in the middle," he explains as he touches his stomach.

So I touch my stomach, and quite with delight and surprise, smile and answer him, "Yes, then I am hungry."

He then offers me food and explains to me the necessity of regular nourishment. He further explains that not only humans need food, but all living things do. I like that he is so wonderfully knowing of such things.

Time flows gently around and through us as we share company and I learn more about the world and we learn about each other. Then, it seems we most naturally fall in love with each other and the world.

As I listen to him and watch him, there seemed to be something dark, almost black, underlying his glorious vibrancy. He doesn't appear to notice it of himself, so I mention nothing.

We seem to have been walking for miles and hours. As the sun starts its dreamy descent back into the cooling sea, I feel myself becoming hungry once more and say so.

Smiling at me he says, "We should find shelter for the night is near."

"Shelter?" I question his word. His face tenses.

What can he say? He wants to protect her, love her, keep her fragility away from them all. He will be, can be as guilty as the other. No, he must tell her, but how?

"Shelter keeps you warm and safe. It's a form of protection from the elements or harmful presences," he states.

"I fear nothing," I say. Then I stop and tilt my head in concentration. And look directly at him and ask, "Should I fear?"

He looks at me strangely with confusion amidst all his colorful emotions.

"Yes," he answers reluctantly. He had been steering them into a protected glen of trees, grass and flowers during their conversation. "Sit down, please," he motions. "I have a story to tell you."

I do as he bids me and listen eagerly. I greatly enjoy learning. He begins. His voice a sing-song tone, captivating my full attention and engaging both inner and outer senses.

"A long while past, a babe was born. A child of incomparable beauty and energy. The parents were less than content though. They feared greatly for their daughter's life. She seemed to draw energy to her, absorbing it, and then radiating it from herself to color those around her. Being in her presence took away fear, doubt and sadness."

As he speaks, I can see the babe in my mind's eye; I can see his words.

He continues. "She gave completely of herself, never asking for anything in return. The parents knew suitors would come, and though they were not eager to accept any, they knew also that men do not well accept a rejected betrothal offer.

"And as the babe grew into a beautiful and grace-filled young woman, she continued to be the embodiment of pure love and joy. None of the suitors were a match for her, and she turned them away, even as they each vowed to return with more exotic gifts to swoon her. She smiled upon them as she sent them away, sending them her energy to gladden them as they left.

"A deep feeling of loneliness, of being too special and different, began to grow in her heart. She was not oblivious to the whisperings in her home-keep, surrounded by those she trusted and who loved her, that for all her beauty and light, her destiny would be tragedy and aloneness."

I can see the tears on the young woman's face, and upon the faces of her parents. I can feel the emotions of the rejected suitors. I myself have tears falling upon my own face, but do not realize it. He continues.

"She began to draw into herself, trying to realize who she was and what her life meant to her world. She had always felt special here, surrounded by safety in her home-keep, but now she craved the freedom and openness of the meadows and surrounding forests.

"Then one morning, a rainy morning, a glorious dawn lighting up the sky, she found herself drawn to walk alone over the grassy field. She felt in tune with her surroundings, the grass, the dampness, the birds, the gentle wind, the smell of the damp soil under her feet. So intent was she upon her experiencing of the natural world that she did not notice the man who watched her from afar. He must have understood the range of her senses, and stayed just beyond. And when he was sure that she was too far from her home, he invaded into her realm of senses."

A cold shiver runs up my spine causing goosebumps like a blanket all over my skin. I feel the sun's warmth being hidden. My storyteller continues.

"She greeted him pleasantly as he quickly approached her. He seemed most polite and asked if they might speak a while. He wanted to hear her unique view of life. Of course she agreed. As they sat upon a nearby felled tree stump, she began to feel the strength of this man's emotions."

I can feel them!

"And as was her nature, she absorbed them, for she had had no teacher to have given her instruction on how to shield and protect herself. For, she had only ever experienced absorbing the emotions of others and then changing them and calming those emotions and returning back warmth and love to those around her. But this man was like no other she had met. He took advantage of the door she had opened for him through her generosity of spirit. Once she opened the door, and he was in, he locked the door shut. The young woman would never return to her parents or home-keep, she was impriso..."

"NO!" I scream at my storyteller. I jump up and I run and run and run. I will not go there again - the story, his story, is my story. How did he know? Is he the "him" he has been speaking of? No. I know with clearness in my heart that he is a friend. Realizing that, I stop running. Looking around, I have run deeper into the forest. It is uncommonly quiet, the only movement being a persistent cold wind.

Where have I come from? What direction shall I take to find my storytelling friend? I don't even know his name. I send out my senses, opening myself to the ebbs of the world around me, confident that I can find him near. Instead, a blast of cold!

"Aaah!" I give a startled cry. When suddenly I recoil back into myself for fear of separation, and then I see before me with my eyes a looming figure of a once great man.

SHERRY LYNN CAMPBELL

"So we are re-united," he says in a haughty, husky voice. The voice seems to have an unused quality to it.

"So it seems, but you will not like the outcome," I reply back, smiling. I am not afraid. I have remembered who I am, and what I have been through. Those thoughts strengthen me. I continue, "I am not a bauble for you to dawdle with. I am a free and whole entity unto myself." I can feel my power surging and swelling inside of me and flowing and surrounding me in loving protection.

He chuckles at my courage, stupidly. "Oh my dear, but you are. I am the Great King, and you are my Queen Gem. I will take you back." He says smugly.

"No, you won't!" a third voice joins the conversation. One I recognize as friend, only now there is no music in his voice.

The Great King does not turn around, using intimidation as a weapon, or at least trying to, "So you would take her for yourself? Does your lust burn so deep you are willing to die? Fool." Now turning to face my friend, the once great king practically spits the words out, "She already belongs to me. I hold the essence of her soul, all her memories and knowledge."

"You hold only her past," my friend replies. "She has a future. You do not. I will not try to deny her that future as you would." And as my friend speaks, he himself begins to shimmer. My heart goes out to him, sending a flash of green light energy. I can see him sway a bit as he stands there, as if a wave has floated through him. He has accepted me and the warmth and strength I have offered to him. He turns to look at me, and then I feel my own self sway in the waves of his spirit and soul energy that he shares with me. The strength and passion of his emotions are a healing tonic to me. Blues and reds swirl upon my skin and through my hair, shining even through my white velvet gown.

"Noir," The Great King roars as he names him. Noir keeps the flow of energy to me, but he has shifted his gaze back upon the king. The king continues, "So you choose now to give your power freely? Fool," the Great King roars with a harsh laughter. "You open yourself, now I can take you both. My own happiness will be found in keeping you apart from her for all time and space."

And as the Great King raises his scepter, a golden web begins to spin outward and a caging net begins to form around Noir. Fury rises within me. I flash fiery reds, oranges and yellows. Noir can no longer move as the golden cage is descending over him. His own colors begin to diminish and fade, but only slightly. He fights still. Without thought, but with great purpose, I step into the path in front of Noir, raising my own hands in a motion to ward off the descending web.

In all my life, I have never experienced rage. This is not rage of my own but rather thrown upon me by another but I understand anger. And I use the weapon my enemy has given freely to me and amplify it back upon this Great King who seeks only to harm.

I unleash all the energy I have been storing and repurposing for my lifetime into that angry emotion that this enemy can understand. In myself, I recall all the love and kindness and peace and joy, building up a light field protecting myself and Noir. I know the power of Love and Wonder. I know that this Great King so filled with greed and hate cannot stand in this light. The golden web begins to fracture, then falter and then fall away. The king staggers back, stumbling over his own feet. He shrinks from this Light of Love, but I will not dim it.

He yells to me, "Lis," he cries out a name I recognize as my name. "You are mine." Then his voice cracks like thunder into oblivion.

The flurries of colors slowly become a warm glow filled with shades of pink, gold, and green. As I turn to face Noir, I realize the colors of my own emotions are mixed with his. I don't notice when he puts his arms around me, but I accept the embrace and lean into his warmth and security.

Where the Great King had once stood is now a pillar of colorless stone. There are small flecks of sparkle off the stone, giving a false sense of worth. I and Noir, hands clasped, turn and walk away into the forest and lose ourselves in each other.

Many nights have since passed, and we both have travelled great distances. We sit close to each other on a beach as dawn breaks.

"Noir," I ask, as I scrunch my toes into the cool sand, "Long ago, we were named, but I've always felt like my name is incomplete. Is there more to my story that you know?" There is a long pause in our conversation as Noir stares out at the waves crashing upon the shore. He shifts his body and sighs.

"Yes," he answers. "But by telling you, you will be completely free of all men. Of even me."

"Noir," I say, kinda leaning in and gently bumping into his shoulder, "I will never be free of you. You are part of my whole. You make me whole."

He nods weakly, reluctant to continue. Another deep sigh, but he does continue. "Your full name is Opalessence. You are the embodiment of a jewel, a gem of vision and of love. The Great King strove to have his artists copy you, recreate the mystery of color and energy. But, they of course were all unsuccessful. So, he set out to trick you into vulnerability and then trap you. Then, he had you fashioned into a pendant and wore you as an ornament upon his breast. He used your power for his own pleasure. He drained your energy to a point of almost complete darkness and loss of color. At that point, he took you off, not wanting any other to see the grayness he had caused due to his appetite for power. It was then that I was able to steal you back away from him."

"Steal me back? Had I known you before?" I ask, my confusion building.

"No, but I knew you. I had never seen you before, only had felt you, your spirit, when you were encased. For you see I was encased once before as well. I was there upon his ring-finger, and as he would reach up to touch you, I understood what had happened. I became drained much faster than you and then I was discarded. Once discarded, I reverted to me in this form, and I knew I needed to free you."

"You set me free? How?"

"I'm not really certain. I had you in my hand. I wandered into the forest, and I was so tired. Nightfall had already arrived. I laid down and fell asleep in the moonlight. When I awoke before dawn, I realized I was no longer alone. I found you once again in this form, as you are now, laying beside me. I figured it best if you awoke alone. You had not aged in this physical form from the day you had disappeared. And, when you did awaken from sleep, you seemed carefree and unhindered of worry. I thought that hopeful," he finishes.

I sit there in quiet contemplation, trying to comprehend what he has told me. It doesn't feel untrue. I am curious. "Noir," I say, reaching out for his hand. He offers it willingly. A peaceful quietness falls over us.

The dawn has become day already. Releasing his hand, I stand up and dust the sand off. I need to do something. I tilt my head to one side and silently asks "What?" to the water, to the wind, to the sky. But, only the wind answers me.

Noir is watching me, aware I am doing something but unsure of what. Then I do something he doesn't expect. I twirl in the sand, as if dancing with the wind. Light and colors are dancing around me as I spin. My light laughter sounds like little bells in the air. I reach down to draw him up and into the dance with me. He feels my joy and wonder.

He loves her so. He feels so loved by her.

I pause our dance, and look at him and say aloud, "I am Love. For you have helped me to see and feel Love's essence." Then I stretch out my arms wide as if to encompass all I can see, and name myself. "I am Opal, and forever a gift to lovers." A tear slowly rolls from my eye, filled with luminous and vibrant colors. A wind arises around us, almost like a cocoon. My whole being becomes one of light and color and he allows himself to feel his own light and color. A beautiful blending of two souls in love. And when the wind calms, what is left are two exquisite stones upon the sand glimmering in the full sun.

CHAPTER 11
What now?

Jow has been shifting her body and causing her little bell to ring, and ring and ring. Greer, hearing the sound of Jow's bell, realized she was awake. She knew she was in his arms. In Forbes' arms. She knew she didn't want to move or have this moment end. She didn't know if these feelings were solely her own, or leftovers from what she had just experienced in a dream. And she wasn't even sure of what exactly did happen. She'd never dreamt like that before. Is that what happened every time Forbes learnt a new story? And if it was, how did she dream with him?

She must have stirred enough to awaken him. She felt Forbes' arms tighten protectively around her. She leaned into that embrace and smiled. She felt whole in a way she didn't understand. And then it was over. She could feel him shifting his body and he released her from his arms. She sat back and looked at him. He had tears running down his face.

"Are you okay?" she asked with worry and concern tinging her tone. In a moment of uncharacteristic tenderness, she reached up her hand to wipe his tears away. But of course, her hands were so dirty that she really just made his face all smudged with soot. Which of course caused her to chuckle at him. When his expression turned to confusion, she sheepishly responded, "Well, I think I just made it worse," she confessed, holding up her dirty hands in her defense. Forbes just smiled at her and shrugged it off.

Now it was his turn to ask, "Greer, are you okay?"

"What just happened?" she countered.

He rubbed his hands across his eyes and said, "Well, I'm not altogether sure. First, I've never kissed anyone ever before, only dreamt of what a kiss was. So, if this is what happens when people kiss, I'm thinking I may have to forego kissing for the rest of my life."

"Ok, I think you are overreacting," she responded. She certainly didn't want to never try that kissing thing again. She took a chance it wouldn't happen every time, and simply leaned in and kissed him squarely on his mouth. He was taken off guard, but he didn't pull away even though both could feel the slight sparking and tingling energy flowing into their bodies. After what seemed a long enough while to prove that they were still awake and alert, she pulled back gently and said, "See. It wasn't just the kissing part. Now we can move on to what else you think just happened." She was practical as ever, he thought.

"Kairos!" she said as she stood up too fast and had to grasp onto the cart to steady herself. Having had more experience with dimension dreaming, Forbes took a deep breath, and used the cart to pull himself up. He stood next to her as they looked into the cart bed.

"Is he okay?"

Greer watched his chest rise and fall with breath. She counted the seconds of each rise and fall and it was steady breathing. Kairos seemed still unconscious, but stable.

Greer turned to look at Forbes and asked bluntly, "Why were you crying? No wait, first, why did you stop so abruptly?"

"Aah," Forbes stalled, and pulled Greer farther away from the cart just in case Kairos could hear them.

When they were a suitable distance away, with no place good to sit, Forbes invited Greer to sit with him in the dirt. She obliged. She wanted to be cross with him, but he seemed genuinely concerned about what had happened. So she let him explain.

"Ok. Ok..." he sighed, moved to run his fingers through his hair, and stopped himself when he felt the bandage there. So he shifted on the dirt a little and then started again. "What do you remember after the first kiss?"

She looked straight at him, and answered, "Opal." His mouth dropped open. She felt like they were meeting for the first time all over again. So she smiled and said, "You're not going to fall asleep in your cheese and bread again, are you?"

He chuckled, remembering that first unexpected meeting and said, "No." Then he continued, "So you experienced that dream story with me?" To which she simply nodded in the affirmative. Then she asked,

"Don't you think we should look in your backpack? I'm pretty sure we are going to find two stones - one light, one dark, but the same."

Forbes agreed with her. Went to retrieve his pack without disturbing the wounded Kairos, and returned quickly. He opened his pack and laid out the contents since they had met: a small golden arrow detailed with four roses, a small blue gift box tied with a white ribbon, a tiny birdcage-style bell, and newly added were two beautiful luminescent gemstones—one white opal and one black opal.

Greer and Forbes looked down at these mysterious story tokens. Greer asked the question, "What do they mean?"

"I don't know, but I think I'm supposed to," Forbes answered.

"Ok, back to the first question, why were you crying?" Greer asked with a tenderness that surprised even herself.

He felt vulnerable, exposed. But the tone in her voice let him know that she was as well. "I suppose because for the first time in my life, outside of dreaming, I feel what love is," he paused here, and then looked up and into her face before continuing, "because of you Greer."

Greer continued to meet his gaze. She felt hot, and cold. Her eyes were getting blurry because there was water filling them up. Her voice and throat felt tight, but she managed to get the words out, "I am scared." And then her eyes spilled over. Forbes moved closer to her and drew her protectively into his arms. He whispered into her ear,

"I am too." He held her until he knew she had gathered her composure again. Once he released her, he smiled as he watched her instinctively rub dirt into her hands and then onto her face, masking any sign of weakness.

Nothing had been resolved. But they knew and trusted that they were in this together. He would tell her later about Aeolian. He wanted to see if he could tie this together in his thoughts. It must all be connected.

"Do you think you're up for continuing to travel a bit more?" Greer asked Forbes. All he wanted to say was no, but he knew the safest plan was to move on. So he nodded in the affirmative. And with one more check of Kairos, they were once again on the move.

They walked for hours in a comfortable silence through the moonlit darkness over an even terrain. Eventually, after the night was mostly spent, Forbes broke the silence.

"Greer, I think I need rest, and to relieve myself and I am hungry. I think we made good inroads to getting away in this nowhere." Greer turned to look at him and respond non-verbally, feeling more tired than she wanted to admit, and nodded in agreement.

The topical terrain had begun to change a bit from the random rocks, boulders and shrubs to a sandier soil, and the air had taken on a new quality, sort of salty. There seemed to be a little more breeze than they had been used to as well.

Just as Forbes had noticed it, so had Greer. "Forbes, I think we are getting closer to a place my father had told me of, a great body of water and cliffs." Seeing his need to relieve himself, she smiled and added, "go ahead and take care of yourself and then we can talk more over a meal." He didn't waste any more conversation and went about his personal business.

Greer checked on Kairos. He seemed to be still asleep, and the bump on his head had become smaller and less angry-looking. She didn't like that he was still asleep. But, she and Forbes needed to eat and care for themselves if they were going to be able to care for Kairos as well.

Greer very carefully removed what she needed from the back of the cart for their camp and meal. After making sure Kairos was still securely settled, she moved onto Jow. Jow always welcomed her attention. She unhitched Jow from the cart and let her wander a bit. Greer never worried about her roving too far away. Greer set her attention back to making camp. There were no stones to use around her small fire. The texture of this ground was gritty and fine and she sort of molded it with her hands into a circular ridge that would ring in the fire. After she was sure it was high enough, she used her flint stones to start the fire and set up the tripod for their cooking pot.

Forbes returned just as she was finishing this, and let her know to go take care of herself while he picked up the meal making from here. She felt so grateful to have companions. She felt so grateful to feel love again. She nodded and walked off in the direction she had seen Jow head. A kind of calm peace had settled on her.

Forbes watched her walk away and thought, she's different now, changed somehow. And as he moved about the camp prepping their meal he thought, *I'm different now and changed somehow*, and in his head he heard a voice that was not his own say, *"Beginnings are boundless."*

He stood very still. Then he moved quietly to place the pot into the tripod above the small fire, and sat down upon the sandy soil.

He calmed himself. He closed his eyes and thought his words, "Who are you?"

A breeze picked up, and swirled around him as he sat. Then he heard "*Aeolian.*" And as suddenly as the breeze had begun, it stopped.

Greer walked back into their camp, leading Jow and saw Forbes just sitting there, eyes closed, in front of a now boiling pot, unmoving. "Forbes? Are you awake?"

He opened his eyes and looked at her and replied, "Huh??"

She continued, "Looks like you fell asleep sitting up. But I think whatever you prepared is ready. Then you can have a proper sleep, lying down." She teased him.

Should he tell her? "*No,*" was the answer to his thought in his head, so he coughed and said, "Yeah, guess I am more tired than I thought."

After their meal, and tending to Jow, Greer urged Forbes to go to sleep. She would take the first watch. She felt revived a bit after the meal, and wanted to work on her project for Forbes before the blanket he was using wore away completely. He willingly followed her suggestion.

Greer quietly gathered her supplies under the guise of tidying up. She could recognize when he was asleep after traveling so many nights together. She had also retrieved his pack. She wanted to see the items again, to match up against her stitching. She had the quilt piece she had made to represent herself and her story of Beginnings are Boundless, a black scrap that she had stitched a sky full of stars upon using yellowish thread. She had her forest green scrap with the golden-rose arrow for Meridal and Robin Hood; she had a tan piece, which she had placed a smaller square of sky blue and then embroidered over with white to make a bow for the Christmas story; she had another shade of blue scrap with tan thread to form an open birdcage in the shape of the small bell for the Easy Way OUT. The last two items were the opals. She held them in her hand. They were so filled with color. How could she capture that in thread? She looked at her available choices of scrap fabric and searched through them until she found a strip of white and a strip of black. She then sewed the two halves together and, using all the colors of thread she had, she embroidered little dots throughout both sides of black and white color. She finished as the sun rose in beautiful shades of pink and lavender. Quite pleased with her efforts, she carefully tucked away her workings, returned the items into Forbes' pack, and replaced them carefully onto the cart. She took her pillow, since her blanket was on Kairos, and laid down beside Forbes to help her stay warm. She nudged him to wake him up. As she felt him stirring awake, with a smile, she herself fell asleep.

Forbes realized, as he was awakening, that Greer had quite uncharacteristically snuggled in beside him as she fell asleep. He smiled that kind of quirky smile he sometimes smiled in contentment. The world, his world, was different now. He moved himself up into a sitting position, as he leaned against the cartwheel for support. He noticed the colors in the sky announcing this new day, and again felt that kinda awe in that even the sunrise seemed to echo his joy. Unexpectedly he had a little shiver, realizing that the mornings were still a bit chilly, and that this morning in particular had a bit more moisture in it. He removed his own blanket and laid it over Greer. Then he moved to restoring the dung fire, and getting the morning meal going.

As he moved to the back of the cart, he was mindful to take care around Kairos. As he shifted things about to get at what he needed, Kairos moved. Forbes smiled at him. Kairos looked a bit confused and tried to move his hand to his head, but they were still tied down to secure him in the cart while they moved. Kairos mistook this and panicked a bit and started thrashing about.

"Whoa, whoa!" Forbes tried to calm him. "You're okay. Not a prisoner. You were injured and knocked out. We secured you to keep you safe as we travelled." Forbes' words seemed to help Kairos put his memories back into a timeframe and help him realize he was not in danger from Forbes or Greer. As he relaxed, Forbes started working on "unsecuring" him from the cart-bed.

"Ok, you need to get up slowly, you might be dizzy," Forbes advised. Kairos could hear the concern in his voice and was happy he trusted the advice. Forbes helped him to sit up, then scooch to the end of the cart and stand up with his help. Once Kairos felt steady, he indicated that he very much needed to relieve himself. Forbes said with a smile, "Be careful, call out if you need help."

Forbes realized the need for Kairos would be water and food. So he got busy with the fire, and taking care of his companions' needs. Surprisingly, Greer slept through it all.

CHAPTER 12
Discovering Ourselves

After Kairos had awakened from his unfortunate accident with the fighting staffs, he noticed that everything about his companions seemed to have changed. Their attitudes towards him, each other, everything. He was confused and delighted by it all. He was now a cohesive and trusted part of this small, odd group. He was given more freedoms, both personal and around camp chores.

Greer was instructing him in new skills such as sewing, and responsibilities for Jow, and even, to his surprise, actually teaching him fighting skills.

What surprised him the most about all of this was his own daily conversations with the cow named Jow. He thought that maybe they were crazy, or had magical arts, but now he and the cow were having conversations as well! Did he have magic powers now too??

He talked to Jow about everything, and asked her questions, and somehow they were communicating. Occasionally he would catch Greer smiling to herself as he had the cow-to-person conversations. He noticed Greer looked different with a smile. So he asked Jow about that, "Why does everything feel different now?" Kairos watched for Jow's response, which was a long breath out and flick of her tail. "I know, it's probably not that much to you, but it feels like it to me. And Greer seems less fierce with a smile." Jow shifted her feet. "So, you agree with me. Ok, good." And then Kairos moved to brushing her, and their conversation took a pause.

The pause in their conversation gave Kairos more time to wonder in his head how his fortunes had changed so dramatically. He had a sense that they were getting a lot closer to wherever it was they were headed. The landscape had changed to something he had never experienced. The ground was all gritty, and sometimes your feet would sink even when the ground was dry. It definitely made gathering the dung a lot easier. And sometimes when you held the gritty dirt in your hand and the sun hit it, it sparkled. The nowhere they had been in was turning into a somewhere! Every day since he had become, at first, an unwelcome member of this group, to one that was now valued and trusted, was something to be excited about.

He thought about these changes a lot. Training and companionship during the day, and the benefit of listening to the Storyteller's stories at night. Yeah, he wanted to be a Carter when they got wherever they were going. It seemed to him that Greer had the best of everything. Freedom, friendship, autonomy, and the ability to talk to cows. Oh, he forgot to add, pretty fierce fighter, as he rubbed his upper thigh and remembered he had learnt never to let your guard down.

He still wondered though if the first story he had heard from Forbes had truth to it—that Greer and he were not the same sex. Something about Greer seemed so different from him and Forbes. And Greer was the dirtiest person he had ever been around, with an odd habit of just rubbing dirt on their own face. But Kairos shrugged it off, because he was so happy to be here.

One morning after their meal, Forbes and Kairos were clearing up, and Kairos asked a question, "Why does Greer purposefully rub dirt on his face? I don't get it."

Forbes was expecting a question, or many questions, on the seemingly different behaviors of Greer. Often times Forbes and Kairos would walk away together for their relief time, offering each other privacy, but Greer always went alone. Forbes would grow stubble on his face, but Greer never did. How old was he? And why did he seem to be in charge if he is so young as to not even grow facial hair? Forbes knew that Carter's scheme to disguise Greer as a male would only work if there wasn't prolonged time spent too close to her.

Since Forbes had been expecting these questions, he had been devising some responses. No time like the present to try one out, he thought to himself.

"Well, I think because he traveled alone for a while it helped him to hide his scent from wild animals that might prey on him," Forbes tried to answer as nonchalantly as possible.

Kairos thought that made sense, and with his own hand still slightly damp from cleaning the dishes, he picked up some dirt and smudged it around his own face. Forbes, barely able to contain his laughter, asked, "What are you doing?"

Kairos answered, "Hiding my scent. I want to keep safe too!" Forbes gave an agreeing nod and then added dirt to his own face and neck. Then Kairos and Forbes finished up their cleaning chore.

Greer who had been on the other side of the cart had overheard their conversation and witnessed the result. She had to duck back away from the cart a bit and laughed as quietly as she could.

Later in that week, Kairos was enjoying his training lesson with the fighting staffs. He chuckled to himself that he was making friends of a sort with the wooden poles, which had only recently knocked him out.

"You're getting better Kairos, but stay focused!" Greer's advice brought with it a clean sweep of his legs. He landed with a thud in the much softer sand they are traveling through now. Greer reached down with a hand and an encouraging smile to help him to his feet. She continued, "You really are getting much better, but when you go onto your thoughts, your focus changes. Your opponent, if they are observant, will see that and then boom, down you go."

Kairos nodded his head in agreement with this wisdom. He could hear Forbes' chuckle a bit from where he was making their evening meal. And Jow shook her head to fill the air with her tinkling bells. So Kairos gave himself a little shake and took his ready stance.

Their jousting began again. This time Kairos didn't lose his focus, but Greer did as they both heard Forbes call out in pain by their fire. Kairos had already been set in his motion of attack and his follow-through caught Greer unready. She had lowered her staff a moment before Kairos' swing landed a blow to the side of her head. Greer collapsed like a dropped blanket, all rumpled.

"Oh, OH NO," Kairos' voice raised the alarm. "Forbes, I didn't mean to, she dropped her staff mid-lesson when you cried out, and OH NO." Kairos was rambling words of apology and shock and inaction. Kairos was talking so fast but Forbes heard none of it. He was there by Greer so quickly that it surprised Kairos. Forbes gently tried to straighten Greer, and then he looked at his hand which felt damp and sticky, blood! The voice Forbes used next, Kairos had never heard come from him before. A commanding voice.

"Kairos, cleaning rags. Water. Pillow. Wound kit and bandages." Kairos seemed frozen in fear of what had happened. Forbes commanded again, "NOW." And with that word, Kairos sprang into action.

After retrieving all of the supplies Forbes had listed, he knelt down beside Forbes for any new instructions. He thought Forbes looked so calm, when his own insides were turning over and over. Forbes stayed focused on Greer. He had her laid out now and it was definitely her head that was bleeding. He felt like his whole life was dependent on what he did next. He had no idea what to do next. He kept pressure on the spot of the bleeding, but it didn't seem to be slowing down.

Forbes spared a look at Kairos. The youth was white. And then Kairos fainted. Forbes knelt there, with Greer bleeding, Kairos passed out, and had no idea what to do. He said out loud, "I need help," and closed his eyes. And then a voice not his own answered, "Help is here."

He opened his eyes, and standing there in front of him was Aeolian.

He looked and blinked, and shook his head to make sure he was truly awake. Aeolian smiled at him and leaned close, touching his forehead with her outstretched hand and he heard the word, "Remember."

Aeolian watched him slump down into sleep. She had no time to explain to a distraught Forbes the hows and whys of it all. Aeolian had already crossed so many lines that at this point, what was one more? She told herself rules were rules and the gray areas were guidelines. The words inscribed on her rainbow obsidian heart ring comforted her, "Love will not obey." And again she wondered as she did on that sea cliff so long ago, what was a Guardian worth if they only guarded but never helped?

Erenow/Greer needed help.

The youth Kairos also lay in a slump of his own making. She didn't need him waking up either. She reached over to touch his forehead gently and said out loud, "Sleep well."

Then, she turned to her charge with a determined task of healing. It had all been going so well for Greer, but even the best-planned ideas go sideways, just one of the many great mysteries of living life.

Aeolian positioned herself in a kneeling pose at Greer's head. She calmed her feelings. She calmed her thoughts. She reached out from her heart for the Field of Love, which was her source of being. When she felt the connectedness, she took her hands and placed them on either side of Greer's wounded head without quite touching Greer. One deep breath in, one deep breath out and then Aeolian focused her energy through her hands and said, "Heal."

A kind of soft light emanated from her hands and into the area around Greer's body. And then it seemed, to anyone who could see, that Greer herself glowed. A soft tinkling of bells let Aeolian know that Jow approved and was grateful.

The light had a soft warmth and then subsided as did the light. Greer heard a voice in her head that was not her own, but familiar nonetheless, say, "Rise."

She opened her eyes and sat up. She was surprised she was covered with a blanket and that her pillow was nearby as well as a bloody rag and that both of her companions were slumped asleep around her.

"What? What the heck happened?" she asked, mostly to herself, because obviously neither Kairos nor Forbes was in any condition to answer. Since neither had moved to the sound of her voice, she reached out to Forbes' body as he was the closest. She couldn't rouse him, but she recognized the now familiar signs of story dimension dreaming. So, she moved on to Kairos.

"Kairos, wake up," Greer said as she shook him gently. He stretched out, and then yawned, and sleepily asked, "time to wake up already?"

To which Greer replied an enthusiastic, "YES."

Kairos did wake up then. And started spouting all manner of apologies at her, to which she confusedly responded with, "Kairos, what are you talking about?"

Meanwhile, Forbes, as commanded , was remembering....

Childom

—— · •●• · ——

L ost among the clouds is how I feel, yet I know that my feet still rest upon the Mother. The fog is so thick, so complete – I walk as one within a dream.

Why had I chosen tonight to commence my perilous journey into adulthood? If I linger any longer though in Childom, I will never leave—to be forever young is what so many desire. Well, not me! I want to grow up, live and be wise.

I have already broken so many governances, will one more make any difference? As a younger youth, Childom had indeed been a paradise - play, play, play. Never a worry, never a care. As a maturing youth, I had discovered the Forbiddens. Having never before been denied, I eagerly sought these out. The Forbiddens consisted of History, Fables and Legends, old maps of the Mother, Biology, a variety of stimulating subjects mostly in book or video formats. Basically, they are anything that causes a mind to quest, a voice to ask, a soul to yearn. I have many questions and yet I must always keep my voice silent and my soul in check.

Interaction among the youths has always been encouraged, though no close bonds are allowed to be built. Also, the youths are divided into three classifications: young youths, amateur youths and mature youths. I suppose there is a reason for this separation. It is not clear to me yet, but when I am wise I will know.

We are always working on group security and cohesiveness, not individual development. At every transfer stage there are tests of mind power and brain development. Those with vibrations outside the parameters go away. Not very many have ever come back, at least not in the same classification level.

The classification levels interest me enormously. No one knows or has memory of the Before. How did we become youths? In my reading of the Forbiddens, I discovered interesting data that suggested how it may have happened, but well...all of us that I have seen were all the same, no external parts I mean.

My biggest question is, what is a Man? or Woman? The pictures show that they have similar qualities as us, but they are very different. Another puzzle is, where did the Forbiddens come from? How come I can find this information if isn't supposed to exist? And how are our separations in these different classifications managed? And who and where are the mature youths?

My departure from the general philosophy has seemed an easy path for me, so deciding to leave Childom has also felt easier than I had expected. I wonder if I have been noticed as unattendant yet? The food chute went straight back to the kitchen. Strange that there are no people here, only machines. I am glad I had hopped out of the chute in the kitchen area since I have no desire to see where the food scraps end up.

The kitchen area has large clear holes in the wall, which are solid. There is a whole other place on the other side of the wall. I press my face on the clear wall and then pull back; it is cold. I press my face against the coolness and, breathing out, realize that the clarity has changed and become cloudy. As I pull my face away from the glassy surface again, the clarity returns. How do I get through?

I put both my hands, palms flat and equidistant apart on the clear surface and give a good, solid, pressured push. I feel a little give, so I try again. This time I brace my legs and feet and push with my whole self. The clear wall opens up just enough for a curious soul like myself to crawl through. I land upon the Mother, with what the atlas had called fog surrounding me. I don't know how long I have been walking, but in my heart I believe I have left Childom behind.

Just wandering along though, I discover I am hungry. Nourishment had always just been provided. I am not sure what I should do to feed myself. I am also tired. I begin to wonder if I am truly prepared for the path I have put myself on...and worrying thoughts overwhelm me. Not knowing what else to do, I sit down. The best way I know to quiet my mind is sleep, so I lay down and will myself to sleep.

Part 2

"Remember," a voice says.

When I awaken, the fog is gone. And I am disoriented. Where am I? Where's the cart? Greer? Kairos? Am I dead? I had a dream about a youth escaping...Have I changed from dimension dreaming to dimension hopping?

I start to feel a little panicked...and then, a voice from behind me asked, "Are you hungry?'

I turn to face a stranger, but they feel familiar somehow. Cautiously I ask, "Who are you? Where am I?" To my surprise the slightly older than me man cooking breakfast chuckles a bit, and then responds, "Forbes, come and sit down. Eat and then I'll answer those two questions, and all the other ones filling your head. And yes, Greer is fine and so is Kairos. Sit. Eat."

Feeling like I should be reluctant, I also realize I am so hungry. So I do as I have been instructed because now I am curious as well, to which the man offering food says out loud, "Hmmm, curious is good."

Realizing someone can read your thoughts is unnerving, so I try to quiet my mind, be here and now and eat.

Once I am through my second helping of food, I begin to feel a little more settled, less afraid and more interested in why I am here. But I want some ground rules, so I suggest, "Being that you can read my thoughts and I am unable to read yours, how about we try to simply address the spoken questions?" The man across the fire slightly bows his head in approval of my suggestion. As I finish up the last of my meal, I observe him as well. He appears to be older than I, but only by a few years. He wears facial hair, very well groomed. His clothes are made for traveling, but of high quality and craftsmanship. He has a camp, but I can not see any cart upon which he would carry such gear. I sit my plate down on the ground to the left of me to indicate I am finished eating. I rub my hands together and then make eye contact with him. "Please tell me your name. You seem so familiar to me, somehow."

He smiles, "You have a good memory for details Forbes. My name is Koan. Aeolian sent you here."

His answers only bring up more questions, "Where is here?"

"Here is where you began your journey as a storyteller and then eventually learned to dimension dream. You see Childom didn't suit you. You wanted to know and learn and grow. So we let you find a window out, and when you did, you went through. Not every soul yearns for what you yearn for, and the ones that do help make the world what it is."

"Is this where Greer was before the Carter found her?"

"No, Aeolian brought you into that 'story' with the character you know as Erenow. Erenow wasn't supposed to be there. But, Aeolian has a loving heart, and her actions complicated things a bit. Erenow chose to become..."

"Greer!" I blurt out. It all made sense now in my head.

"Very good Forbes. You always were top of your class."

"Ok, okay. But, why am I here now?"

Koan rubs his fingers through his thick hair, and sighs a bit, which kind of reminds me of myself, and continues, "Well, Greer was unintentionally hurt pretty seriously, and Aeolian couldn't let it be after everything with Erenow, and Greer was doing so well, and well your feelings and her feelings, and then Kairos comes along...," Koan stops speaking, realizing he's rambling on. He looks over at Forbes, who is sitting there staring at him, mouth agape, and then asks, "What?"

I very slowly answer with my own question-statement, "You are my Father." At this point, Koan's eyebrows shoot up in surprise, and then even in more surprise because he hadn't known that I have been thinking that.

"How are you shielding your thoughts from me?"

"I don't know. Am I?"

Koan and Forbes both hear their names said in a scolding manner and turn to see Aeolian standing there with her hands on her hips, scowling at the two of them.

··●··

Faraway, Forbes hears another voice calling his name, "Forbes, can you hear me."

CHAPTER 13

Remembering

W ith both hands on Kairos's shoulders, Greer is trying to get Kairos to make some sense of the scene she just woke up to. So she spoke slowly to get him to focus on her, "What are you talking about?" He stopped trying to explain and apologize, and wrapped his arms around her in a very tight hug. This caught Greer off guard. There had never been a lot of touching in her world. Well, she could remember hugging her father, but now Kairos was hugging her in the same manner. What a curious turn of events. She felt proud and privileged to have someone care about her the way she had cared about Carter. So she hugged him back, and assured him that she was okay.

When the hug had run its course, and they pulled apart, she realized he was crying. She dried his tears with the dirt she absently picked up and said he was good to go. Kairos smiled at her so she smiled back.

Then she turned to her next task, waking Forbes.

Kairos said, "I don't know what happened to him. All that blood coming out of you, so I just fainted I guess. Maybe he fainted too?" Greer nodded at him, then moved on to Forbes. She would deal with the so-much-blood comment in a minute. She rolled Forbes flat on his back and then grabbed her pillow and put it under his head. She was surprised and disturbed by the blood almost dry now upon it. She gave him a shake, but made sure she was out of his way should he bolt up as she had in previous mishaps, and said, "Forbes, can you hear me?"

His eyes opened and he said, "Yes." He sat up slowly with her supporting him on one side and Kairos on the other.

Kairos said, "You must have fainted like I did. But look, Greer's okay. I must not have hit him as hard as I thought. All that pressure you were applying worked." Kairos finished, and they both could hear the amazement in his voice. But, the look Forbes gave to Greer let her know something had happened that was different than the scenario Kairos painted.

Greer looked at Kairos and asked if he would get the fire going again. It seemed like a meal was a great distraction. Kairos was all too eager to help, especially at something he knew he was good at. As he was getting the supplies from the back of the cart, there was a brief moment of privacy between Forbes and Greer.

He whispered, "Are you really okay?"

Greer smiled the softest smile he had ever seen her make and nodded yes. Then she helped him up, and said, "See if you can help salvage that meal you were making before you burnt your hand." Then she stopped and moved her hand up to her head where she had been struck and found hair matted with her own dried blood. She realized she had forgotten her own rule while training or fighting—to stay focused. She smiled a smile of irony, and then started cleaning up the mess of supplies that had been pulled out. There was some washing to do.

That night around their dung fire, all their faces smudged with dirt, but bellies full, Jow cared for and all the washing done, Forbes announced he had a new story to try out on them titled Childom.

The next morning, during waking up, preparing for the morning meal, cleaning up the morning meal, caring for Jow and collecting dung, and packing up the cart to move on, all Kairos could focus on was wanting more details and questions about the story Childom.

"Ok, Forbes, so do we all come from Childom? Do you think I was one of the special ones?? And why are there Forbiddens? We have Forbiddens here too, don't we? And why are all the youths neither male nor female? And why are females different? Why do we never see them, and really, only you ever speaks of them? And how do we choose to be one or the other?" The questions swirled around Forbes, making him dizzy almost. He noticed one of two times Greer trying to hold in her chuckling at Kairos' enthusiasm. Greer had some questions of her own about this story too, but trying to get a word in edgewise this morning was more effort than she felt it worth. As she was loading in the back of the cart, with the other two distracted, she covertly checked on her secret project for Forbes. She was nearing completion, and with all the hands looking for things in and out of her cart, she just wanted to make sure it hadn't yet been discovered. To her relief it was hidden and safe where she had left it.

The last thing to add was the dung, so she needed to interrupt Kairos' questioning and ask him to bring the dried pieces to her. He sighed and then did as he was asked. As Greer was holding the bag open and Kairos was carefully placing the recently dried dung, he had a question for her. "Greer, do you remember choosing to be a male? Do you think Childom is real?" He watched her face carefully and noticed that she held her breath a little and raised her eyebrows before she looked at him to answer.

"You know Kairos I have a great memory, but I don't think I can remember that far back. Can you?" was her response.

Kairos seemed disappointed and kicked the dirt a little, "No," he sighed, "I can't remember that far back either. But, don't you kinda wish it was true and that males and females could live together and know each other?" His comment made her smile, a pensive and wishful smile. Kairos was caught off guard for a moment at how different Greer seemed just then.

She answered him, as she turned away, closing up the bag, realizing she gave him a glimpse of her difference, "Yes, Kairos, the world might be much more interesting that way. But for now, "It's a man's world." And she deepened her voice just a bit as she said it and then tied off the contents of the cart in preparation for their day's journey. Forbes who had been covering up the remains of their fire, heard and saw the conversation, and the momentary surprise in Kairos' eyes when he looked at Greer. He knew Kairos could be trusted, but the danger of that trust seemed a heavy burden for one so young to carry.

As they walked in their customary silence, except for the gentle jingling of Jow's bells and the turning of the cartwheels, Forbes' mind travelled back through his last dimension dream. He had a father, a father who was proud of him and cared. That made him smile inside, and he felt bigger somehow. He, of course, realized he had come from someone; everybody did, but most never knew. Again, he wondered at the whys of it all. He was different by design, it seemed, as was Greer. He had a sense too that Aeolian had been the skirted figure he had seen in his childhood as he entered into the Storytelling Guild training program. He also believed there was something more between Koan and Aeolian, maybe something similar to him and Greer. And, if that was the case, then was she his mother? He felt like he was tingling with light at all these amazing thoughts. He wanted to run and jump and twirl and yell with all this energy, but he simply sighed and kept pace with Greer and Jow and looked behind occasionally to make sure Kairos was keeping up.

Kairos was in his head too, and in his heart. He felt loved for the first time. He felt he belonged in a way that was more than just being part of a household. He thought everyone should live this way. What was the word Forbes had used in the story when telling them about the Forbiddens? Family? Yes, it was family. Family sounded right. Kairos felt like this now was his family.

Greer wasn't immune to being in her head either. She thought back to waking up and not knowing what had happened, and Kairos throwing himself into her arms to be held. And comforted. She remembered those times when the Carter would allow these moments. She remembered how safe she felt. How he was home. Forbes had taught them a new concept last night in his story, Family. She liked that word, and what it meant to her. She allowed herself a soft smile, knowing neither Forbes nor Kairos could see her face, but she was surprised by a soft tear that fell from her eye. So much emotion these days now that she had let herself feel. Her family had grown from just the Carter and Jow to Forbes and Kairos and Jow. No one could replace her father the Carter, but Forbes and Kairos were definitely a new home for her. She felt great gratitude for the fortunes of her life, even with the mistake, as Forbes told in his story, "Beginnings are Boundless," about her. But, being a female hadn't robbed her of anything, not freedom, not strength or intelligence or strong will. And, she did realize she was beginning to learn new skills and strengths in grace, acceptance and patience. This time her smile was strong and confident. She was sure that the Carter would be proud of her and how she was finding uses for the lessons of her life.

And she heard a voice that was not her own in her head say, *"He is."*

And with that said, Greer decided it was a good time to take a break and eat their midday meal.

They took a little longer break than usual for a midday meal. They each wanted to talk with each other about all the changes in the landscape, in themselves, and how each of them felt that a great sense of "something new and amazing" was very near.

Kairos had many more questions for Forbes about Childom, and parentage, and why things are Forbiddens, and that his world had seemed out of balance now that he had new information. Forbes tried to help Kairos understand that he didn't have all the answers to his questions and that it's the nature of storytelling to stretch the imagination. He did compliment Kairos on being a good student and enjoyed his inquisitiveness, even if it was mentally exhausting. Of course, Greer wanted to chime in here and there about the different stories she had enjoyed and how they made her feel and think about things in a different way, which of course led to Kairos complaining he hadn't heard as many stories as Greer. Forbes laughed and assured them both that stories are made for retelling.

And as their conversation and meal came to a natural end, the clean up and repacking began. They seemed to move as a well-practiced team and were back on their way toward their exciting new somewhere.

They were not to be disappointed.

Their journey out of the nowhere was finally complete. Before them stood a forest of giant trees with a vibrant undergrowth of flowering plants and greenery. And there were such new sounds for their senses. They stood there together looking at it all. Smelling it all. Listening to it all. And even their skin seemed to be sensing it all. The air had changed dramatically. It had a moisture to it, a coolness. Greer closed her eyes and just let herself feel it all. She opened her eyes, and looked over at Forbes. He was looking at her. Greer felt as though he was both looking right into her thoughts and feelings as well as allowing her to look into him.

Kairos's voice broke the spell, "Do you think it's safe to go into there??"

Greer smiled a very sure smile at Kairos, reached out to clasp his shoulder, and answered, "Yes." And with that she and Jow led the way into the forest of giant red-barked trees and walked into a forest floor filled with plant life.

As they walked, they noticed it wasn't just plant life; there were birds, and insects and small climbing animals moving through the forest minding their own daily rhythms. Sometimes the forest floor greenery would move seemingly on its own. Clearly this forest had many more inhabitants to discover.

Even though it was midday and the sun was at its brightest, the forest felt much colder and darker than they were used to. It was easy to find beams of sunlight breaking through, but they were small beams. As they continued to walk, the air changed again. It went from a damp coolness to having an actual taste - a salty taste. There was a new sound as well, drowning out the other forest sounds.

Greer looked at Forbes, and asked, "Do you hear that? It's kinda like a roar?" Greer and Jow stopped walking.

Forbes stood still and closed his eyes to listen better. He shivered a little in the damp coolness. He could taste the salt in the air as well. He heard a roar and then a crashing sound. The sound paused and then repeated, almost rhythmically. He cocked his head to one side to listen more intently. It seemed familiar to him somehow. He opened his eyes and looked at Greer, "It seems familiar, doesn't it?"

She nodded in the affirmative. Kairos seemed distressed, "What's wrong?? Is it a monster? Are we in danger?"

"No, I don't think so." And with that they all started moving forward again toward the sounds. After a few more minutes of walking, the forest opened up to dunes of sand and an ocean of water.

It was almost as if what they stood before was right out of the dream story that Greer had shared with Forbes. There was an ocean! Forbes must have made the same connection because she and he exchanged knowing glances. Kairos added his own thoughts out loud, "That sound is SO loud! Are you sure we aren't in danger?"

Greer once again, clasped his shoulder and said, "No, I don't think so. I think we've arrived!!" The excitement in her voice was clear for both Kairos and Forbes to hear. No dream, or story her father had told her could have prepared Greer, or Forbes, for the grandeur of this view or of the physical force of the water in front of them. Greer looked once more over at Forbes, she smiled a smile he had never seen before and then took off running full steam to the water's edge. She only looked back once to see if they were following, and then she plunged herself into the water and let the waves knock her about until she was floating upon the water's surface.

Moving the cart through sand this deep wasn't going to be easy, so with the instructions to stay put given to Jow, Forbes and Kairos took off running to try to catch up with Greer. Neither of them understood what was happening or why she ran into the water.

Greer wasn't worried at all. She felt so full of life and joy and had no sense of fear. She didn't know how she knew how to move her body in the water to be safe, but she did. Floating face up there upon the top of the water sparked another memory...of being everywhere and nowhere at once. But that memory floated away as fast as it had arrived. She could hear Forbes shouting from the shoreline, so she flipped her body over and dove under the water, swimming into the shallower shore. She unfortunately took in a mouthful of water which tasted terrible, but that seems to be the only drawback to being in the water. She stood up out of the water to see if Forbes or Kairos would join her in the water. As she stood there closer to the shore than the ocean, little waves of water would come in lapping at her legs and then pull back out. She looked at her companions who seemed to be looking at someone they had never seen. Which in part was true.

Greer didn't understand what they were seeing. She turned around to look and see if there was a monster behind her. Nothing but the wide ocean. She turned back around confused. She smiled at them and motioned with a wave of her arm for them to join her. There was no way for Greer to have anticipated that her momentary joy in the water would have washed away her protective veil of maleness.

Kairos spoke first, "You are a girl!?!" He looked at Forbes and continued, "You said she wasn't a girl. That is not a man!"

Forbes looked at Greer, as herself, no disguise. She was radiant. He loved her, so he just smiled at her.

When she realized that she had washed away her disguise, and Forbes still smiled at her in that way he did and understood he accepted her no matter what, she found a confident voice to answer Kairos. "Yep, Kairos, that's true. I am a girl and I can still best you both in combat. So, who's hungry? Let's make camp and eat," she said, clapping them both on their shoulders as she walked past them, continuing back to the cart. Jow mooed a very warm welcome.

Greer felt exposed. She felt elated. She felt seen. She felt accepted. She felt overwhelmed by all of the questions Kairos rapidly sent her way. He asked one question after another without allowing her to answer any of them. She just smiled at him and went about setting up their camp for the evening and helping Forbes prepare the meal. Kairos didn't know what to do with all his energy and questions, so Greer stood in front of him, grabbed hold of his shoulders and squared him up to face her directly and said, "Kairos, Jow needs some attention. While we get camp and dinner ready, will you take care of Jow?" She said this calmly and with intention. Kairos blinked once, took a deep breath, and then nodded a yes. Now with something to focus on he felt less off-balance.

Greer smiled at him as he and Jow walked off into the forest a bit, and then she called after them, "Kairos not too far, I think this could be a place one could get lost in easily."

He waved back and answered, "If we get disoriented, we will follow the dung fire scent back."

Greer nodded her approval of his answer and thought, "smart lad." Feeling more confident, she returned to the camp. Forbes wasn't by the fire. She looked around, maybe he had gone off to relieve himself. She heard a noise at the back of the cart; it was Forbes. He was crying. He was holding something tightly and close to his heart. Greer moved to see what was wrong.

"Are you hurt?" she asked, moving in closer to examine him. That's when she noticed what it was he was holding. He had found the pieces of embroidered fabric she had been working on for the quilted blanket as a gift for him. She was confused. She had been working on these pieces to make him smile, not cry. With her hand placed gently on his closest shoulder to her, she asked quietly, "Why are you crying?"

Forbes didn't answer at first. His throat was so thick with emotion. His heart was beating so fast. And his eyes were all blurry from tears that he couldn't clearly see what he clutched in his hands any more or her face. But, her soft voice soothed him and the smell of her and the dung fire meant home. He finally took some deep breaths and then asked, "What are these?"

Greer, trying to lighten the mood, said, "Oh, well, those are to help repair your tattered blanket," she answered. Then continued, "It was supposed to be a surprise. A thank you for all the stories you have shared with me. I don't know if you can tell what they are," she paused, "but, if you hand them to me I can tell you."

Forbes handed them to her, and as she took them into her hands and then turned to lay them out on the cart-bed, Forbes surprised her by grabbing her up in his arms and planting a very meaningful kiss on her lips. She pulled back for a minute, worried about being seen, worrying about falling into a dream story, and then threw all caution to the wind, and returned his kiss with equal intention.

Jow and Kairos had been returning to camp, but had stopped abruptly at the sight of the two of them in an embrace. A very different kind of embrace than when he had hugged Greer. After getting over the shock, a wonder-filled, happy smile came upon his lips and face. Jow mooed and shook her head and bells. Kairos said to Jow, "Yeah, I think you're right. I think they are in love." Kairos would have never known or understood love as well as he did at this moment if it wasn't for the time he had spent with Greer and Forbes and Jow. He looked forward to learning more about it every day in every way.

Kairos wasn't sure, but he thought he heard a voice in his head that wasn't his own that said, *"Beginnings are boundless."*

Afterword

They had made a comfortable little camp at the edge of the forest and the beginning edge of the dunes. They were learning that everything they needed seemed to be provided by the forest or the ocean.

Greer had taught both Forbes and Kairos how to swim so that they could all be safe in the water. They were learning about the tides and the daily movements of the ocean.

Forbes had given Kairos his own whittling knife, since he had, in one of his many dimension dreams, come across one as a story souvenir. He taught him how to use it carefully since they'd already all had their fair share of mishap injuries.

Kairos seemed like a boy born anew. He took to scouring the beach shore looking for items that could be of use to them. Greer had nicknamed him the "beachcomber." Kairos especially liked finding all the smooth pebbles on the beach.

He had found a really smooth and perfectly shaped oval black stone, and had been using his knife to etch a design on it. Greer and Forbes had seen him working on this and wondered what he was making. So at their next evening meal, they asked him about it.

Kairos explained, "Well, since we got to the forest, and found the ocean, and you two fell in love and kissed," he paused because they both blushed as well as reached for each other's hands. Then continued, "I heard a voice, and I wanted to remember what it said." Kairos noticed that both of their demeanors changed immediately. They let go of each other's hands and sat up straight, encouraging him to go on. So he did.

He held out his stone with its etched "B" upon it. Greer took it in her hand first, then handed it to Forbes. His craftsmanship was impressive, but they were more interested in his why.

Forbes asked, "What did you hear?"

Kairos answered, "Beginnings are boundless." He was a bit worried that maybe he had done something wrong, but both Forbes and Greer smiled huge smiles and then started laughing and crying all at the same time. Kairos was so confused until Greer, pulling herself together, and moving to sit next to him and returned his stone, said,

"Yes, they truly are." And then gave him a hug.

· • ● • ·

The End for now.
Their story continues in The Storyteller's Circle.

Characters

The Carter: a man who carts. He is a wanderer. He's not an outcast per se, but chooses to keep his own company.

Jow: name of the cow who wears a bell. Her name means to ring a bell.

Greer: her name means alert, watchful and vigilant.

Forbes Kaylynn: his name means headstrong.

Kairos: his name means opportunity, synchronicity or mythic timing.

Aeolian: the Guardian whose name means relating to or arising from the action of the wind.

Erenow: her name means before this time.

Koan: a Guardian whose name means a paradoxical anecdote or riddle without a solution. (In Zen, it is used to illustrate the inadequacy of logical reasoning and provoke enlightenment.)

Author's Note: the names and their meaning listed above are found and defined in these sources:

1. Carter, Greer and Forbes as defined in What to Name Your Baby from Adam to Zoe by Maxwell Nurnberg and Morris Rosenblum, 1984

2. Kaylynn is found in the Llewellyn's Complete Book of Names by K.M. Sheard

3. Jow, Kairos, Aeolian, Erenow and Koan are all words which have been used as names by me and are defined in online dictionaries as in Merriam-Webster Dictionary

Preview of The Storyteller's Circle: Love Is The Key

Greer, Forbes, Kairos and Jow having settled themselves into a new somewhere, are building a new life together. Kairos feels like he's entered into a world full of magic and discovery. He not only explores the beach and the forest, learning about the animals and rhythms of nature here, but also who he is and what being part of a family feels like.

Greer has never stayed in one place so long, and can't believe how big their camp is growing. She also is finding herself lost in the wonder of love with Forbes, and in mentoring and caring for Kairos. She not only is experiencing what those feelings feel like, but she's also noticing other changes with her own body that she doesn't quite understand.

Forbes isn't exactly sure of what to do with himself every day. He's always been around people, but not so intimately, and not just the same people. He's not questioning his love for where he is or who he is with, just how he, himself, fits into it all.

All three are being guided by Guardians, Aeolian, Koan and Jow. And, new Guardians are on the way to help them each develop their full potential. The little trio won't be a trio for long with newcomers, of every sort, showing up. Life is about to get even more interesting and potentially even more perilous. But, they have each other; that much they know is Truth. And the story-dreams keep coming...

Author Bio

Sherry Lynn Campbell is a storyteller and children's book author as well as a life-long reader.

Her favorite genres have always been Fantasy, Mystery and Science Fiction. She enjoys all yarn crafts, including crochet, knitting, embroidery and needlepoint.

Her love of storytelling and song-making for the children in her classrooms led to her first three books: M is for Mother, F is for Father and The Five Little Snow Kids for early childhood-aged children and their families to share together.

Since retiring from teaching, Sherry has been following "her own inner child" to explore and write new stories for a wider audience. The Storyteller's Quilt is her first book in the upcoming young adult or young at heart trilogy of the Storyteller's journey.

This book, The Storyteller's Quilt, began as a dream, a dream of writing one story that would be good enough to share. Then Forbes introduced himself to her on the page and helped her put her stories together so that Greer, and other characters, would come alive on the pages. These characters and their journeys are now yours to experience, enjoy, and carry with you.

When not writing, she is inspired by finding wonder in nature, especially at the beach, in a forest or on a mountain. She is living happily ever after in San Carlos with her very own true love.

You can follow Sherry on her website: www.WonderEddy.com

Reviews

"Reading *The Storyteller's Quilt* felt like sitting with friends, wrapped in nostalgia and purpose. Each chapter will awaken something inside you. The stories are real, rich, and full of heart. I was reminded how deeply connection matters, and how much wisdom is available in our everyday lives. This book is a living quilt of truth and tenderness. It was moving.   Trust me, you'll come away from it feeling deeply grateful and inspired."
—**Gary L. Fretwell,** Fretwell Solutions

•• ● ••

"True to its title, The Storyteller's Quilt is a patchwork of short stories, focused on themes of female empowerment and agency, that are woven together by the tale of an itinerant storyteller and his found family. Each story is a gem in its own right (in one case, literally), and together they form the glittering tapestry that is Campbell's first YA novel."
—**Craig Young**

· • ● • ·

"This book immediately captured my attention. Where are they? Who are they? Where are they headed? The three main characters are intriguing: Greer, the foundling who grows up to lead them on; Forbes, the dreamer and storyteller; Kairos, the young attendant; and not to be forgotten, Jow the cow. They are stitched together in a magical way, much like a colorful quilt.   I look forward to the next adventure."
—**Kathleen Frazer**
Jewelry Designer, moonsilverstudio.etsy.com
Quilt Crafter, New Zone Gallery, Eugene, Oregon

· • ● • ·

"What a joy to discover The Storyteller's Quilt! Sherry Campbell has crafted a beautiful novel filled with strong, compelling characters who journey through both familiar and fantastical landscapes. The imaginative narrative "turns the tables" on the reader, who cannot help but see themselves on this journey of discovery and love."
—**Janet Hall**
Chief Financial Officer, Stanford Alumni Association
https://alumni.stanford.edu/about/leadership/

· • ● • ·

"The Storyteller's Quilt is a winding narrative with lots of twists and turns to keep you captivated. This book is a lovely journey to settle into."
—**Becky Moller**

"The Storyteller's Quilt twists and turns, weaving widely varying patches of adventure together in an earnest frame. It's a stitching together that puts love first, despite the complexities of the society that Sherry Lynn Campbell has put together, and the whims of time, dreams, and powerful beings hiding just out of view of the reader and the characters. The patchwork is simultaneously a labor of love and pointed, unexpected musings on lives lived and the choices that define them."

—**Jay Fry**